Margaret Ann's Diary

A Paranormal Mystery

Robert W. Birch

Margaret Ann's Diary

Published by

PEC Publishing

429 Grand Ridge Dr.

Howard, OH 43028

ISBN 10: 1499500955

ISBN 13: 9781499500950

This is a major revision and "sterilization" of the erotic novel by Robert W. Birch, titled Margaret's Diary: An Erotic Ghost Story published by Carnal Desires Publishing (2008).

Margaret Ann's Diary

A Paranormal Mystery
By
Robert W. Birch

Chapter One

"When are you coming to bed?" It was getting late, and Cathy Riley sounded half asleep as she called out from the small bedroom of the modest ranch-style home.

"I'm trying to get a start on this new novel I've been obsessing about," Kevin responded as he shifted his weight on the hard wooden chair in front of his computer desk. "I can't come up with any ideas for a decent plot or interesting characters." He had taken a few literature courses in college before dropping out in midstream during his junior year, but he hadn't had much luck as an aspiring author. At twenty-eight, he worked for a local moving company, which kept him in good physical shape and offered a flexible schedule.

"Come to bed and snuggle. You've been at that darn computer ever since you finished dinner."

"Just a couple more minutes, hon." Kevin stared at the blank screen for another three minutes and then shut the machine down. He watched the monitor flicker and turn dark. "Darn," he said out loud, expressing his frustration. He hadn't even been able to come up with a place to start. "I'll brush my teeth and be right there." He walked to the bathroom, turning off lights on his way. Tonight he hurried his brushing, instead of following the dental hygienist's advice to brush for a full two minutes. He loved Cathy, his twenty-five-year-old wife of three years, and enjoyed their snuggling when his brain was not worrying about points of view, action tags and an assortment of other guidelines that can bug any unpublished author obsessed with getting things right. Tonight, however, his mind was blank. Cathy's petite body felt warm and cuddly as he spooned up behind her.

"I love you, Kevin Riley," she whispered.

He kissed the back of her neck. Her hair ticked his nose as he sniffed her skin. She smelled good. "Love you too, hon." His body began to relax, but all of a sudden his mind switched on and his thoughts raced.

A mystery, yes – that's it! I'll write a mystery. But romance sells. Maybe I should write something mushy. Okay, murder and a lot of passion and love. Or I could do an historical novel, but there's no time to do the research. I can't get my head around romance in the seventeenth century. Darn, there's got to be something – maybe a paranormal story about vampires., but I wouldn't know where to start.

"Are you going to sleep?" Kathy asked.

"Sorry, love, but I just can't get in the mood tonight. I can't stop thinking about that darn novel."

"It'll just come to you some day. Now give me a kiss and let's sleep."

Kevin lay awake for another half hour wondering about the basic genre of his unwritten novel. He had already written a romance, but all the editors told him that it lacked spice and would not appeal to the predominantly female readers of romantic stories. His second attempt was a more erotic story, but the editors all thought it lacked romance and was too pornographic. He would try one more time, and if he couldn't publish this one, he'd quit trying. He figured three strikes would mean the game was over. Before finally drifting off to sleep, a crazy thought ran through his head. *One more rejection and I'll take an art class. Maybe I can make it as an artist.*

* * * * *

On waking to the sound of their alarm, both occupants of the bed found that the arrangement of their two bodies had changed. Cathy was snuggled up behind her husband and their Siamese cat Buster was curled up at the foot of the bed.

Kevin hit the button that ended the loud buzz of the clock and stated the obvious. "Time to get up, love." Having stretched voluptuously, Cathy inhaled a deep breath of air laced with the aroma of the purple lilacs blooming just outside the open windows. The high wooden fence surrounding their yard allowed them to sleep without closing their drapes, except for those mornings when they could sleep in. The sun had not yet risen, but the morning's soft predawn glow provided ample illumination within the room.

Ignoring the morning's light and the now silenced alarm, Cathy wiggled her warm body against her husband's strong back. He rolled to where he could kiss around her closed eyes and down her nose. Their lips met, soft and loving. "I love you, Cathy," he whispered, "but I really don't have time to play this morning. Can I get a rain check?"

"Only if you promise to be good," she teased.

"I've got to get going," he muttered, and slid out of bed, accompanied by Buster, who hit the bare hardwood floor with a thud and scampered into the bathroom ahead of the man who he knew would fill his water bowl. A few minutes later Kevin arrived back in the bedroom. "Buster's got fresh water. Now, I've gotta get some coffee." Bending down, he kissed Cathy on the forehead. "You did set the timer last night, didn't you?"

"No, I thought you set it," she replied without opening her eyes.

"Oh, darn, you usually do it."

She grinned. "I did. I was just kidding."

"Never, ever, kid about my morning coffee." He leaned over the bed and kissed Cathy on the cheek. She looked so pretty curled up there with her eyes closed. He was tempted to climb back in with her, but he had to settle for one more kiss. He was already thinking about the busy day that lay ahead.

She smiled without opening her eyes. "Going to bring my coffee?" It was a needless question, as Kevin had been bringing her coffee every morning for the three years of their marriage. He'd put the cup on the counter by the bathroom sink where it could cool while she showered. On this morning he felt he needed to get to work early, but he did leave her coffee on its designate spot.. Since he was not destined to become a prizewinning author overnight, he was forced to work hard for a living. He had settled for driving a truck for the moving company. When with friends, he'd often complain about the low pay, but he'd then add that at least lifting furniture was good physical exercise. Cathy would usually then joke that she hadn't married him for his money. She'd just wanted his body.

Kevin was finishing his second bagel when Cathy walked into the kitchen. She was a beautiful woman, and she was not the least bit shy about displaying her beauty to her husband. She obviously loved how he looked at her. As she walked toward him, he turned toward her, and his eyes traveled down her body. Smiling a devilish smile, she ruffled his short brown hair. She then bent and kissed him on the forehead, before moving to the kitchen counter.

As she began refilling her cup, Kevin moved behind her and wrapped her in his strong arms, being careful not to make her spill her coffee. He kissed her on the back of the neck. This was one of the many spots on her body that he loved. "You look and smell wonderful this morning," he remarked. "I've got lots of stuff to load and then unload at an auction house. I'm not too sure where I'm going or what I'll find, so I really do need to get an early start." Had it not been summer, she also would have been hurrying to get to the elementary school where she was employed as the music teacher.

"I hope you'll think of me today," Cathy said softly. "When do you think you'll get home?"

"I'm not sure, but probably not until after dark."

"You'll be on the road most of the day?"

"No, the house isn't far away, just in Bedford. Over the next couple of days, we need to move everything out of it. The widow who lived there died a few months ago, apparently leaving no heirs and no will. It seems that she still owed the bank a lot of money from the refinancing of her home, so the bank's going to auction off the house and all its contents. Today I need to load up all I can carry out. I'll bet that over her ninety years, she probably collected a lot of junk."

"Don't try to lift anything heavy."

"Don't worry, hon. Tomorrow Bill will be with me, and we'll get the big stuff. Today's going to be pretty uneventful."

"Does anything exciting ever happen on the job?"

"Other than finding someone's collection of porn? No, it all pretty routine." Kevin filled a thermos with coffee, grabbed a banana and picked the three largest oatmeal raisin cookies from a puppy-shaped cookie jar on the counter.

"Lunch?" Cathy asked.

"Fruit and grain." He kissed her. "I love you, pretty woman. I'll be home for dinner."

"I'll miss you." It was already warm outside, and the forecast was for temperatures to reach into the high eighties. "Drive carefully, and try to stay cool," she called out.

"That won't be easy," he yelled back. His truck was not air-conditioned, and he anticipated some hard work ahead. During the summer he cut his hair short, but that did not help much on hot days. He waved one more time out the open window as he backed out of the drive. *Darn, I sure love that woman,* he thought as he drove away. *I'm glad she asked me to marry her.*

* * * * *

The house of the deceased woman was in the small town of Bedford, thirty miles from his home. Kevin thought he was familiar with her neighborhood, but he double-checked as he approached. "Turn left at the stop sign," the female voice of his GPS instructed.

"And then we'll get dirty," Kevin answered back to his microchipped traveling companion.

"Turn right at the next intersection," the voice directed, unresponsive to his lewd proposition.

"Thanks, baby," he replied, spotting the large two-story Victorian style house at 620 Mayflower. Pulling into the driveway, he studied the white shingled house with its slate roof, decorated gables and fancy brackets under the eaves. Then he looked again at his work order to compare the numbers on the porch column with the numbers on paper. Once during the prior year he had parked at the wrong house and entered an unlocked front door, much to the surprise of an elderly couple and their golden retriever. He was thankful that the man was not armed and the dog not a pit bull, but he had nonetheless learned to always double-check addresses.

After making one final check of the house number on the key tag, Kevin unlocked the front door and walked into a dim, eerily quiet entryway. Without thinking, he flicked the light switch on the wall, only to discover the obvious. The electricity had been turned off. It was as though the death of the occupant had brought death to the house. Some sunlight, however, came into the living room window through sheer lace curtains, once white but now torn and yellowed with age.

Kevin looked around. By a wing-backed arm chair stood a floor lamp with a tasseled lampshade. The ornate end tables flanking a tattered couch supported matching brass-based lamps, the fabric shades of which had become discolored over time. A small round table reposed in front of the couch, and on it rested a book with a worn cover. Lifting the book, Kevin read the title out loud: "The Collected Works of Henry Wadsworth Longfellow."

Hmm, he thought. *Maybe if I can't write a novel, I could write poetry. To rhyme or not to rhyme, that is the question.*

Just then he heard a faint noise that sounded as though it had come from the second floor.

"Is anyone there?" he called out. Walking to the foot of the stairs, he called out again. "Is there someone up there?" There was no response, but he decided that he'd better go up to see for himself. No one else should be in the house this morning. Slowly, he climbed the stairs and paused in the dim hallway at the top of the steps, commenting to himself about the warmer temperature of the second floor. "Anyone up here?" He listened for a response, but there was only dead silence.

Walking down the hall, he passed a bathroom filled with the colored sunlight streaming through a beautiful stained glass window. The old-fashioned tub, poised high on its clawed feet, and the pedestal sink reminded him of the age of the house and its last occupant. Towels still hung over the towel bars. *How did that old lady get into the tub?* he wondered, and then noticed an enamelware wash basin sitting on top of the toilet seat. *She must have resorted to sponge baths,* he thought, addressing his own quandary about her bathing. *Maybe one of those home care agency people came to help her wash.*

Suddenly he heard another faint noise, sounding as though someone or something had moved a chair. Bewildered, he stood frozen for a minute. "Who's there?" he finally called out in the direction of an open door. There was no answer.

Moving cautiously down the hallway, he peered around the frame of a door. The bedroom appeared empty, except for the expected furniture. "Is anyone in there?" he asked. He had to sure, but the only sound was that of his racing heart, its beat audible in his ears. Stepping into the empty room, he looked around. The bed, higher than most modern beds, was neatly made, although a layer of dust covered everything. There was no indication that anything had been moved in months.

It must have been a rat, or maybe a squirrel or raccoon that somehow got into the walls.

A thick, leather-bound book lay open on the nightstand, face down on a lace doily. Curious, he lifted it to discover that it was a handwritten diary. From the pages that were open, he read a couple of entries dated nine years earlier, about the woman's husband and what appeared to be the last days before his death. He hit the automatic dial button on the cell phone clipped to his belt.

"Hello," Cathy answered.

"Hi, hon, it's me."

"Are you taking a break already?" she asked.

"I haven't been here long. I've just been looking around. I found something interesting, though. Lying on the stand by her bed was the woman's diary, and it was open to the pages where she wrote about her husband's illness and death."

"Hardly my idea of bedtime reading."

"But it's almost as if she were anticipating her own end. It's almost as if she had prepared herself for the reunion, and this was her way of reconnecting with him."

"Oh, Kev, you are such a romantic. She probably just flopped it down, and that's how it landed."

"No, I think she had been reading and remembering. I think she was reminiscing about her husband." Just then, he glanced across the room and focused on a picture hanging on the wall. "There's a photograph here – one of those old ones in an oval frame. It's of a young couple, and I'm sure it's them. She's sitting, and he's standing behind her."

"Classic position," Cathy commented. "Probably symbolic of male dominance."

"No, there's something unique about this pose." He walked closer for a better look. "He's standing off to one side and has a hand on her shoulder. He looks gentle, and one of her hands is resting on top of his. She's looking up at him, and he's looking down into her eyes. It's beautiful, really, Cathy. I wish you could see it."

"You'll be loading all that stuff, won't you?"

"Yeah."

"Bring the photograph home with you, and the diary too. You've managed to stir my curiosity, and maybe there's something in there that'll inspire you to write a romance novel."

"Good idea, but now I'd better get back to work. There's a lot to pack and the house is starting to heat up."

After saying goodbye, Kevin stepped back into the hallway, where he felt a sudden chill. "God," he yelled impulsively, for he beheld a brief flash of what appeared to be a semi-transparent scantily-clad young woman. She sailed silently across the hall, carrying a towel and disappearing into the bathroom. "Darn," he mumbled, and then in a louder voice called out, "Who's there?" He didn't really expect an answer, and there was none – only the faint sound of what sounded like water running into the tub. He moved slowly toward the open door and looked in. The sound ended, and the room was empty.

He hurried down the steps, down the first floor hallway and out the door. Stopping on the front porch, he braced himself against a column of the porch roof. His whole body trembled. *What the heck was that?* he asked himself. He reached for his cell phone, but hesitated. How could he describe to Cathy what he had seen, if he wasn't really sure himself? And how could he tell his wife that he was so scared he almost wet his pants? He decided he would just have to get himself composed and go back in. He had to do so.   He had a job to do, and he needed to finish before the temperature hit its peak.   His boss would understand if he said it was too hot to finish, but not if he said he was too scared to even start.

Mustering his courage, Kevin walked back into the house. It seemed warmer inside than it had before, but he still trembled. *I've gotta do the second floor first,* he thought. It was always good to get the top floor finished while he still had plenty of energy for repeatedly going up or down the stairs. In addition, he knew that once the sun got really warm, the upper floor would heat up first, adding to his discomfort. He had get moving.

He gathered up a half dozen folded cardboard boxes and several padding blankets he had left on the porch. Halfway up the steps he paused and listened. There was just silence. He finished the climb. He stopped again in the hallway, but on hearing nothing, he walked into what must have been a guest bedroom. In this room there were two twin beds, two high-backed wooden chairs with wicker seats, and a vanity dressing table with attached mirror and padded bench. The room smelled old.

From the tables on either side of the beds, Kevin gathered up a small lamps with milk glass bases and dusty cloth shades. Carefully, he wrapped each lamp in the padding he had carried up, and placed them in a box. He gently lifted three original watercolor paintings from the nails that had held them for years, noting how their outlines remained on the faded flowered wallpaper. He checked the drawers in the vanity dressing table. In one, he found only an old glass perfume bottle, a vintage hair brush with tortoise shell backing, and a matching hand mirror. In the larger lower drawer he found eight hair rollers. He guessed that they had no value, but his job was to pack and not sort, so he threw them into the box. Someone else would decide what would go up for auction and what would be discarded or donated to Goodwill. The two drawers on the other side were empty, except for one that seemed to have been lined with old newspaper, cut from a page showing a corset ad.

Kevin was moving toward the bedroom closet when he heard that sound again, coming from the bathroom – the same sound of water running into the tub. His heart pounded in his chest as he ran into the hall and toward the sound. As he entered the empty tile-floored bathroom, he felt a cold breeze and was met with total silence. "Darn," he muttered out loud. "Who are you? Where are you? Show yourself." He waited, shivering with fear, but he was also now quite curious. *Who was or is this beautiful woman?*

Chapter Two

Not seeing the ghostlike figure in the bathroom where he had heard the sound of running water, Kevin Riley turned away from the door, determined to complete his assigned task. To get to the guest bedroom he had to pass the one with the high bed: the one in which, he assumed, the widow had died. Passing the door, he felt a cold breeze, which prompted him to look in. A semi-transparent figure of a woman in a flowing nightgown seemed to float across the room.

"I saw you," he called into the room. "There's no need to hide." However, when he stepped into the room, it proved it to be empty. *I must be going crazy,* he thought. *The heat's gotten to me. This all has to be in my head!*

Seating himself on the bed, he opened the thick diary to its very first page, and read aloud the beautiful handwritten introduction dated November 3, 1936. *"This is the diary of Margaret Ann Ashley, begun on my eighteenth birthday, three days after my betrothal to my beloved John Percy Morgan."*

Kevin closed the leather-bound personal journal and walked to the wall, where the framed photo of the two hung. "Hello, Margaret. Hello, John. The two of you make a lovely couple." He lifted the photograph from the wall and turned it over. There on the back in what appeared to be a man's writing was the date: November 3, 1937. "Your nineteenth birthday, Margaret," Kevin said, addressing the woman in the picture – the woman whose apparition he recognized as hers. He looked closely at the picture, focusing on her left hand that rested on John's. "Married, I see," he said to the young woman in the photograph. "It was a short engagement, Margaret, and that makes me wonder if you were a virgin. Or did you perhaps become pregnant and had to marry?"

A thud that sounded behind him startled Kevin. When he turned, he saw that the diary had fallen off the bed where he had placed it. Picking it up, he looked at the pages to which the book had opened. Silently, he read an entry dated December 25, 1937.

I need John so badly that I have been unable to sleep, I am saving myself, but I have encouraged him to set an early date for our marriage. We have decided that I shall be a June bride, and we have picked June 1st as the date. I am eager to join with him, for I know he is feeling desire every bit as intense as mine.

"That was just an accident," Kevin said out loud while looking down at Margaret's diary. "Or," he added looking at the photograph, "were you answering my question about your virginity?" Hearing a soft, girlish giggle, he turned, half expecting to see Margaret standing behind him. However, the room was empty.

"This is weird," he said to the void. "I'm either totally bonkers, or you're a real ghost, and a pretty one at that." There was nothing scary about the apparition, and Kevin was beginning to feel that he knew this woman who he recognized as the woman in the photograph. "I've got to get back to work. I just hope your wedding night was as exciting as Cathy's and mine." He was about to lay the diary back onto the night stand beside the bed when he experienced a sudden and uncontrollable sneeze. In the process of handling the convulsive sneeze, he missed the little table, and the diary fell to the floor.

Picking it up, Kevin looked at the pages to which it had opened. Silently, he read the entry for the second day of June, 1937.

What a night. I was afraid and excited and shaking from both. However, John was so gentle in the way he held me, assuring me that I could choose how we spent our first night together. I was too embarrassed to undress in front of him, so I did so in the bathroom behind a closed door. When I came out in my long pink nightgown, he was already in bed. I did not realize until I climbed in beside him that he was naked.

Kevin stopped reading and looked at Margaret in the photograph. "Tell me if you want me to stop reading. It's apparent that you weren't expecting anyone else ever to read what you were writing in your diary." Kevin waited, but there were no ghostly indications that the writer wanted him to stop, so he continued to read.

John touched me in soft and gentle ways. No wonder I love this man so!

Kevin took a break from reading and looked around. The bed's headboard was solid, with a rolled top and dark walnut finish. There was no footboard. The mattress was double: smaller than a queen or king size. *I hope that you two liked to snuggle*, he thought. Glancing at the diary, he pictured Margaret and John in bed.

That image brought a response. "Wow, you two," he said aloud to the two pillows at the top of the bed is if they were the young couple in the photograph. "Judging by what's in your diary, I surely think that all your inhibitions must have melted away." Again he heard the soft giggle, but did not bother turning. He knew no one would be there.

Turning back to the diary, but decided not to continued reading. He stopped himself, as he was certain that if Margaret's ghost had a need to share, she would somehow send him a message that would get his attention him. He had work to do. Just then his cell phone rang. It was Cathy.

"Hi, hon," she said. "I just called to see how things are going."

"I'll tell you all about it when I get home. I've been thinking about you."

After they exchanged goodbyes, Kevin turned his attention to the guest bedroom. Having loaded numerous boxes, he made repeated trips down to his van, each time carrying back additional empty boxes and padding. He had been curious about the tower room, but upon entering it, he found that it had obviously become a storage area. His attention was first drawn to the shapely dress form. The narrow waist and the thick layer of dust indicated that this form had been used by Margaret during her younger years. As he walked by it, his hand caressed what would have been a real woman's waist. He was not surprised to hear once again the soft giggle.

"If you were alive today, Margaret, I think you would have been a very naughty young lady." Another giggle came: the same voice but from a different direction.

In this room he found stacks of colorful hat boxes containing fancy hats, some of cloth and some of straw. A variety of ribbons and bows adorned each. A pile of shoes reposed next to an umbrella stand holding a half-dozen umbrellas. Old pictures with ornate frames leaned against wallpapered walls. On opening the heavy lid of a large wooden trunk, Kevin found only one thing: a garment wrapped in tissue paper. He parted the paper, but decided that he wouldn't remove the contents, as it was clearly a white wedding dress: Margaret's wedding gown. This would now be over seventy years old. Looking up toward the ceiling, he promised, "This will never be auctioned off to strangers. Cathy and I will keep it and protect it, along with your diary and the photograph of you and John on your nineteenth birthday."

Kevin spent the remainder of the morning loading up whatever he could carry out from the tower room and the two bedrooms. He ate his snack – the banana and three oatmeal cookies – while sitting on a wooden chair at a wooden kitchen table covered with flower-patterned oilcloth. As he drank coffee from his thermos, he looked around. The old gas stove was obviously the original one, but it was still in remarkably good shape. The sink had apparently been replaced, and the refrigerator appeared to be from the seventies. Pots, pans and iron skillets were scattered around on countertops. Stacks of cups and dishes suggested that in her later years Margaret had been unable to reach the cupboards. He opened the back door to allow in fresh air. He was admiring the decorative screen door when a squirrel jumped up onto an empty platform of a birdfeeder.

"Sorry, fellow, but the lady of the house isn't home."

The squirrel looked at him as if to say, "I'll check back later," and then scampered away.

After he finished what would have to pass for lunch, Kevin focused on the parlor. A number of lamps were carefully packed. A wooden magazine holder reposed next to an easy chair, in front of which sat a padded footstool. Both were covered in a now-faded floral print fabric. The magazines in the holder were all from the seventies and eighties. *Collectors could want these*, he thought as he packed them.

He then turned to a tall, roll-top desk. Sitting in the wooden swivel chair, he rolled up the top. To his surprise, the surface was covered with piles of photographs. They appeared to be in no order, although a bottle of dried library paste and a box of adhesive photo corners suggested that at one point, Margaret had planned to get the pictures organized and into scrapbooks.

This could be a challenge for Cathy – sorting these into chronological order. He turned several over, noting that most had been dated. Some listed names and or places. *Cathy's a visual person, so she'll love arranging these,* he ruminated. He looked at a picture of Margaret in which she appeared to be in her thirties. *Margaret, we'll finish the project you had started, but tell me. In this picture your waist is so thin. Were you wearing a girdle, or were you really that shapely?*

For some reason, his eyes moved to the three small drawers over the desk top. A piece of paper protruded from one. Opening the drawer, he took out a yellowed slip of paper that proved to be a receipt from a department store that had opened in 1908, but had gone out of business years ago. The first item on the list was a corset, described as having "no boning." It was further described as a one-piece garment with brassiere and girdle and garters. Also on the receipt were six pairs of silk hose and a pink chemise.

"You are a very clever ghost, Margaret, but what the hell is a chemise?" No sooner did he pose his question than he felt a cold breeze blow across the back of his neck. Turning, he was surprised to see a flimsy piece of cloth draped over the back of a loveseat. He hadn't noticed this pink garment before. Walking to it, he knew that this was Margaret's answer to his question. He lifted the silken chemise and commented, "Ah, like a petticoat, except shorter." This time the giggle seemed to come from a source just behind him. He spun around quickly, but was alone in the parlor.

"This is really spooky," he said. He then continued placing the photographs into a separate container. "This box goes home with me."

* * * * *

It was after six o'clock when Kevin pulled in the driveway. Cathy met him at the door. Without speaking, they hugged and kissed. Then she asked, "How was your day?"

"You won't believe it, love, but that house is haunted."

"Yeah, sure, and England is just a myth."

"No, listen to me. I'm serious. That house is haunted by a beautiful nineteen-year-old named Margaret – the 90 year old woman who died there – but in the apparition, she's much younger."

"Come in out of the sun, rest, and I'll fix our dinner. You're delusional."

"I don't know how to make you believe me, but I did bring home Margaret's diary, wedding dress, photo collection and that photograph I told you about – the one of her and her husband John. Everything's in this box."

"And what're we going to do with all that stuff?"

"Well, I'm sure that the diary will make for some interesting reading. It will be fun sorting these old photographs. The picture of the couple would look nice hanging in our spare bedroom, and the wedding dress we'll preserve in a respectful way. That was a very special day for her. She was innocent when she married."

"Probably most women were back then. In what year would she have married?"

"1937. She was both excited and scared."

"She told you this?" Cathy asked skeptically.

"She wrote it in her diary."

"You read her private journal?"

"I think she wanted me to. I asked her to stop me if she wanted me to stop."

"Sit down, kick your shoes off, and I'll bring you a cold lemonade." Cathy stepped behind the chair where he sat and rubbed his neck and shoulders. "Just relax, now. After dinner we'll talk about this – after you've cooled down, unwound, and filled your tummy."

"I'd like to read a little from the diary after dinner. I know you'll enjoy getting to know Margaret through her writing."

Cathy picked up the framed photographic portrait of the couple and studied it. "I don't know about getting to know her, but I'd sure like to get to know this hunk. What did you say his name was?"

"John. John Percy Morgan."

"Well, John Percy, what're you doing after dinner?"

Kevin chuckled. For a moment he thought he heard the soft giggle of a woman, but he ignored it, since Cathy didn't seem to hear it. "Maybe I do need to relax and unwind a bit. But let's see what we can learn about this couple after we eat and get the dishes cleaned up." He kicked off his shoes, sat back in his chair and yawned. "Early to bed tonight."

"Promises, promises," Cathy teased.

Cathy had prepared her famous lasagna that she served with red wine and warm garlic bread. A green salad accompanied the main dish, and fudge brownies, still warm from the oven, shared the dessert plates with a generous scoop of vanilla ice cream. As the pair ate the dessert, Cathy told of her shopping adventure with Julie, a friend.

"And what did you buy, pretty lady?"

"Just a couple scented candles."

"Ahhh, I'll not smell then as well as you will."

Together they shared freshly-brewed coffee and a bit more banter about shopping with Julie before tackling the pots, pans and dishes. There being just the two of them, they rarely used the automatic dishwasher, reserving it for those occasions when a large meal with friends or family meant that more of everything would need to be washed – dishes, glassware and cutlery, plus the ever-present pots and pans.

Kevin carried the remaining plates and glasses from the dining room into the kitchen, with Cathy trailing behind, carrying their half-full coffee mugs. She sat at the kitchen table as Kevin began rinsing the dishes and silverware. He didn't notice when she left the room or when she returned, but he heard her begin reading from the diary. "I just opened the book, and this is what she wrote on January 1, 1937," she informed him.

"Last night John and I went to the movies to see Errol Flynn and Olivia de Havilland in Charge of the Light Brigade. We were out by eight o'clock and back to his apartment by half past the hour. John is such a wonderful kisser. I do like the way

he touches me, even though I never let him go below my waist. If only we were married! I must be patient until then."

Cathy took a sip of her coffee. "So, Margaret was hot to trot, but her conscience took over." In reaching for her coffee cup Cathy nudged the pudgy diary and a couple of pages flipped over. She picked it up. "Wow, listen to this January fifth entry, Kevin!

"I have been thinking about why I restrained myself on New Year's Eve, because I really wanted my beloved to know me as no man has ever known me. I think it was my conscience that stopped me. I recalled the preacher preaching about lust and the mortal sin of premarital fornication. As much as I wanted to, I just could not allow myself to go all the way."

"I'm sure glad you didn't have a guilt attack that night I carried you into my bedroom."

At that moment a cold breeze blew across their kitchen and Cathy noticeably shivered. Both heard the chuckle, and both registered surprise.

"Who the hell was that?" Cathy asked.

"Margaret, but what the hell is she doing here?"

"Could she have come with her diary, or maybe the pictures?"

"I don't know, but do you believe me now? Do you believe that Margaret is a ghost?"

"What I want to know is whether or not I'll get to see John naked."

Both were startled by the sound of their front door slamming, even though it had been closed and locked since Kevin got home.

"I think you've made Margaret jealous, and she's gone away mad."

"I don't know why, but I have a feeling that she'll be back after she stops feeling guilty about sharing her thoughts and her man with a sexually liberated woman. I don't know all the reasons she's still stuck with being a ghost, but I'll bet there's something stopping her from joining John."

Backing up, Cathy bumped the table, jarring the diary so that more pages flipped. "I think she's back. Let's see what she's telling us on January 28, 1937.

"My best friend Alice started flirting with John at the soda shop today, and I became jealous. I was angry with her and with John also, for he seemed to enjoy her attention. Then I started thinking about it and realized that Alice was my best friend, and I had always wanted the best for her. I love John and I had always wanted him to feel good about himself. They were just playing, and I knew that she would not try to steal him away from me. After we finished our sundaes and she went home, John and I would remain together. In fact, I even started feeling good about my friend's finding my John attractive."

"Isn't she a creative ghost?" Kevin asked, turning from the sink after drying the last of the silverware. "She manages to answer questions. At her house, she even directed me to the location of a receipt for a purchase of a corset and some silk hose."

"That's pretty personal stuff, young lady," Cathy said, looking down at the diary. "I'm jealous, and I'm going to stomp off mad." The brief cold breeze and soft giggle let Cathy know that Margaret recognized that she was teasing. "I wonder if John is watching too."

"I have the feeling that Margaret Ann's the only one around," Kevin responded, "and she's somehow trapped back on her eighteenth or nineteenth birthday."

"And I'm thinking that for some mysterious reason, either her diary or the couple's photos are the glue keeping her connected to us?" Cathy said.

"Could be the only conduits she can use to communicate with us, but I sense there's something else holding her here."

"I'm hoping that time or Margaret will give us some answers. She seems to have a way of getting in touch, and I suspect she misses John and is eager to join him."

"I think something happened that has her trapped and we need to discover what it was."

"And find a way to free her," Kevin added. "She's only been dead about six months. On her deathbed she thought of John and his death nine years earlier. If she's stuck here, that's a long separation for a couple in love, and she's counting on us to help them reunite."

Chapter Three

Kevin had been sorting through all that was left in the home of Margaret, a 90 year old widow. She had survived her husband John by nine years, and the diary Kevin found told of her devotion to this man. Also while in the home he met Margaret's friendly ghost, who appeared to be woman of only eighteen or nineteen. He became interested in the woman's history and decided to take her diary and a stack of photographs home so he and his wife Cathy could piece her life story together and, perhaps, solve the mystery of why Margaret had not been able to join her husband.

"I'll get that stack of photographs," Cathy said, "and maybe together we can put them in some sort of chronological order. Could be there's a clue in there somewhere. Then tomorrow, while you're back at Margaret's house loading up furniture, I'll read more of her journal."

"Sounds like a plan." Kevin said. He joined her at the kitchen table, and they began spreading out the photos.

"Wait," she said. "First, let's first decide how we're going to approach this. Should we look at the fronts and try matching people and locations, or should we look first at the backs, and use the dates for a chronological arrangement?"

"It might be even more basic than that. Let's first of all sort them into two piles – those with dates and those without dates. Then we'll do the chronological sequencing of the dated ones. Once that's finished, we'll look at the fronts. Hopefully, we'll then be able to get the unlabeled ones into their proper time period."

His wife nodded, and they began turning all the photos over. "You finish this, Kev, while I change into something more comfortable. I'll grab the card table on my way back, because we're going to need more room to spread these out."

Kevin had finished turning all the photos over by the time Cathy returned. She was wearing her short nightie. He watched attentively as she set up the card table, knowing that he should help, but enjoying every perspective of his wife's body as she stooped, bent and twisted.

The now familiar chilling breeze brushed across Cathy's shoulders. For no conscious reason, she reached down and turned over a photo. It was of a young, slender Margaret. Cathy looked on the back, and exclaimed, "1938." She looked again at the picture. "She's telling us that in her day, she also liked to feel sexy – to feel free. Look, here she is in a chemise. It looks like a soft, thin cotton fabric, and if you look closely, you can see the curves of her body."

Kevin turned the photo to the light for a better view. It was of a beautiful, proud Margaret, wearing a chemise having short sleeves and coming to mid-calf. It had a straight-cut yoke, edged, as were sleeves and hem, with a narrow ruffle. "It covers more than your nightie, but I'll bet John got a rise out of seeing her in this. Very sexy."

"Who, me or Margaret?

"Both."

This time it was Kevin who felt the breeze that announced the spirit's presence. He and Cathy heard the giggle and both spontaneously chuckled in response.

"Let's start by making stacks of those from the thirties, forties and so on. Then we can fine-tune."

"Would you believe 1923?" Kevin said holding up a picture.

"I guess that's not surprising. Margaret would have been five years old, if we figure that she was born in 1918."

Kevin moved behind Cathy, so that they could both look at the old picture. *Margaret – June 4, 1923* was written on the back. On the front was a sweet-looking girl with curly blond hair, sporting a large bow. She was dressed in a short, full, checkered dress with puffy short sleeves and a bow in front. Little Margaret held a limp Raggedy Ann doll with button eyes and what was probably thick red hair.

"Cute kid," Cathy remarked.

"She grew up to be a pretty woman," Kevin responded, expecting the cold breeze and soft giggle. Neither came, so he returned to his chair and began sorting.

Cathy had started a stack of pictures without dates on the card table, while Kevin roughly sorted the pictures with dates into the appropriate decade. Once those without a date were sorted out, Cathy helped her husband arrange stacks on the kitchen table. "I had about thirty or thirty-five over there," she stated, "but there must be a hundred or so dated ones."

"And I've not yet seen any from the 1980s, 1990s or 2000s."

"I guess that as you get older, you stop taking pictures. Besides, without children, there are fewer people to photograph or to operate the camera."

"Plus, with old film cameras, you're less likely or able to get the prints developed, and I doubt if Margaret ever thought of going digital. The only camera I found in her stuff was an old Kodak folding bellows type that you probably can't even buy film for anymore. Think of all the changes and advances in technology she must have seen! But I guess, like cameras, we all eventually become obsolete."

"Hey, Mr. Riley." Cathy smiled. "Don't go getting all philosophical on me."

"She didn't have a computer, and I didn't find a cell phone, either."

"Oh my, how did that poor woman ever survive?"

"Wait." Kevin did a double take. His surprise was clearly portrayed in his expression.

"What, Kev?"

"This picture." He held one of the photos out for her to see. "Look, she's holding an infant."

"Could be anyone's."

Kevin took the photo back and looked at it again. "No. From the way she's holding and looking at the baby, I have the feeling it's hers."

"What's the date on the back of the print?"

He turned the photo over. "May 30, 1941. She would have been twenty-three."

"So, that baby would be over sixty-five now."

Just then, they heard their cat Buster cry out from the living room. A thud followed as he hit the floor from wherever he had been perched. By now, Cathy and Kevin weren't taking anything as accidental or insignificant. They both jumped up and hurried into the living room. The cat had apparently scampered out of the room, but the diary lay open on the floor. Cathy picked it up and read the date on the open page. "*May 15, 1941.* That's about two weeks before the picture with the baby was taken. Why am I not surprised?" She then went on to read the entry.

"*Two days ago, as the clock in the hall struck noon, my baby announced that he wanted to come out. John called Dr. Jones, who arrived within fifteen minutes. He confirmed that it was time. I was in labor. He asked John to show him the bathroom, so he could wash his hands, but he came back into the bedroom alone carrying an armful of towels. I was scared, but so happy to have made it full term with this child, having had two miscarriages in the past.*"

"I think they were doing a lot more home deliveries back then, but boy, that must have been risky."

"Kev, women had been having babies for a lot of years before there were sterile delivery rooms in hospitals. Let me read on. This is a long entry.

"*What followed was a long, hard five hours of pain, but I finally was able to push my child out. Only then did I learn that I had given birth to a boy. I cried for joy, as did John. We had decided that if it was a boy, we would name him Stanley.*"

"So the picture was of Margaret holding Stanley when he was about two weeks old."

"Oh, no, listen to this. *May 22, 1941. Dr. Jones says I am not healing as I should. He is afraid I got torn up inside or something. He said he is worried I will be unable to have any more children, but I thank God for giving us Stanley.*"

"Wow, what a mixture of joy and sorrow, but she did get to live a lot of years, and her beloved John was with her for sixty-five of those."

"But Kev, I wonder what ever happened to Stanley. You had told me there were no relatives on Margaret's will and no one inherited her home. This was her only child, and after two miscarriages he must have meant a lot to her."

"And to John. It must be hard for a father to lose his son. It should be the other way around."

"I need a hug right now." Cathy stood up, and Kevin walked to her and held her in his arms. "I don't know what I would do without you," she declared.

"I think it would be much harder for me to be alone. I'm pretty seriously hooked on you, Cathy." Having held her for a few more minutes, he then broke the silence. "Let's get back to the diary. See if you can find anything Margaret recorded that tells what happened to her son."

Cathy leafed through the diary. "There's mention of Stanley. Later, he's called Stan. But mention of him seems to end sometime in '83. I don't see any reference to him after that. I'll check more carefully tomorrow, but let's see if there's anything we can learn from the photos."

They walked back into the kitchen. Buster had somehow slipped in there without being noticed, and was sitting up on the sink counter playing with the water dripping from a leaky faucet.

"It doesn't look as if he messed anything up on the tables," Kevin observed. "Water, leak, drip – A message from Margaret? I can't think of any meaningful associations."

"It was not about the faucet. Look down there." She pointed to the single photograph lying face down under the table.

He picked up the photo and handed it to Cathy, dated side up.

"It just has 1983 here on the back, but it's been blurred by what looks like a drop of water or a tear. Oh, God," Cathy exclaimed when she looked at the front. "It's a picture of a fresh, unmarked grave. Damn, she *did* lose him that year." Tears filled Cathy's eyes. Kevin wrapped his arms around her and held her close. A tear also ran down his cheek. He was going to say something, but he choked up and just held his wife a little tighter.

"I can't do any more tonight," Cathy said. "Let's get cleaned up for bed and just snuggle for a while. I want to hold you, have you, love you, for as many years as I can."

Kevin said nothing, but reached behind him and turned off the light hanging over the table. They stood holding each other in the semi-darkness for another few minutes. Then he led her into the bedroom.

Cathy followed her husband into the bathroom and stood beside him as he brushed his teeth. "I can't get that woman out of my head. Two miscarriages, and then one child and unable to have more – and to make things worse, that son died. What did we figure, around age forty-two?"

Kevin mumbled something in response, but the thought *Real bummer* went through his mind.

Cathy squeezed toothpaste onto her brush, and then looked at Kevin's reflection in the mirror. "I really need to be held tonight. I'm curious about what we might discover tomorrow, but tonight I just need to feel you close."

Looking back at her in the mirror, he smiled a toothpasty smile. He rinsed his mouth and his wife began her frothy tooth-brushing ritual.

"I'm going to go get undressed. Meet you in bed, Hon. It'll be nice to cuddle tonight."

* * * * *

Kevin woke before the alarm sounded and lifted his head to see the time. "You're awake too," Cathy said. "I've been lying here awake for about half an hour."

"We might as well get up, then." Reaching over, he brushed her hair away from her face. Having lightly stroked her forehead, he then ran a finger down the bridge of her nose. Her eyes were closed. Very softly, he brushed across her eyelids, and then over her lips. She puckered and kissed a fingertip. "I need to tell you about a brief but vivid dream I had, but I'm not sure it has any meaning. I remember holding a book of some sort: hard cover, and bigger than a novel. I tried reading the words on the front, but couldn't make them out. I do clearly remember that the cover was yellow and the letters blue. When I opened it up – and this is the weird part – it seemed that the book cried. That's all I remember."

"It was probably just from that stuff with the diary last night," Kevin said. "The only dream I can remember was about moving furniture. You're the scholar, I'm the mover – the brains and the brawn."

"Get your mover body moving, and I go fry you up some eggs. I'll meet you in the kitchen." Cathy climbed out of bed, turned the alarm off so it wouldn't sound.

Kevin finished his quick shower, walked to the kitchen and up behind Cathy, who was standing in front of the stove. He wrapped his arms around her and kissed the back of her neck. They said nothing for a full minute.

"Did you see her? Did you see Margaret?" Cathy breathed.

"Yes, briefly sitting in the chair at the table," Kevin replied. "Was she doing what I think she was doing?"

"What did it look like to you?"

"It looked to me as if she was licking her lips."

"That was my first thought," Cathy said, "like she missed John's lips on hers."

A quick cold breeze caused both to shiver, and then came the girlish giggle. "I guess ghosts can miss hugging and kissing too," Kevin replied.

"But we need to keep moving. You'll need to eat your eggs before they get cold."

"Can I just hold you for a few more minutes? I'm feeling so fantastically good about you," Kevin said, "and I'm feeling optimistic about what we'll learn today. But right now I just want to feel your warm body next to mine."

"Why don't you get our coffee poured? It's time to move on." She turned and planted a big kiss on Kevin's lips and they heard Margaret sigh.

Buster meowed loudly, as though he'd been feeling ignored and now needed his share of attention.

As they finished their breakfast, they heard a knock on the door. "Margaret?" Cathy asked playfully, tightening the sash of her bathrobe.

"Nah, no one that exciting. It's probably just Bill. Striding to the door, still in pajama bottoms, Kevin greeted the middle-aged man who had come to help him move the widow's furniture. "Come on in and have a cup of coffee. It'll just take me a couple minutes to get dressed."

Bill, a large man in gray work pants and shirt, smiled. "Morning, Mrs. Riley," he said as he walked into the kitchen.

"Good morning, Bill. Can I fix you a cup of coffee?"

"Sure, black. Organizing family pictures?" he asked, motioning toward the stack of photos on the table.

"Yeah, you know how easy it is to get behind." Cathy placed a cup of black coffee in front of him in a space that had been cleared between the piles of photographs. "I'm going to have to go feed the cat now," Cathy said. "Have a good day." She walked back to the bedroom, where Kevin was tying the laces of his steel-toed boots. "Don't overdo it today, hon. It promises to be another hot one."

"I'll be in touch, and I'll be thinking of you reading more of the diary." Having kissed her, he left with Bill.

* * * * *

He was not yet to the town where Margaret and John had lived when his cell phone rang. It was Cathy. "Hi Kev. I had to call you. After you left, I went back into the living room and saw Buster knock my family Bible off the shelf. I checked the page where it had opened and found the Song of Solomon and read this passage from Chapter Four. I just gotta share it with you. *How fair is thy love, my sister, my spouse! How much better is thy love than wine and the smell of thine ointments than all spices! Thy lips, O my spouse, drop as the honeycomb; milk and honey are under thy tongue, and the smell of thy garments is like the smell of Lebanon.* Isn't that beautiful?"

"Again I think Margaret is telling us her love for John was as sensual as the love you and I share." He didn't care if Bill heard what he was saying, but the man seemed more interested in playing with the GPS than listening to the phone conversation.

"Yes, I too think this is all telling us through Solomon's poetic verse that Margaret and John had a very loving and very passionate marriage. I just wish we knew what happened to her son, and why, if she died at ninety, she is still hanging around in the image of a much younger woman."

"Well, keep me posted, and if anything shows up here, I'll let you know." Having said goodbye, Kevin focused on the road.

It was 11:30 when he called Cathy. "That book you had a dream about – well, I found it. We were moving the dresser from Margaret's bedroom, and found that the book was in a box that had been stored under it. It's just as you remember in your dream: a yellow, full-sized, hard cover book with the title Baby's Own Book in blue lettering. It's Stanley's baby book, and it follows him up until his fifth birthday."

"Wonderful! I thought that dream must have had some special significance. But what about my thinking that the book had cried in my dream?"

"Are you sitting down?"

"Oh, my, why? What is it?"

"What I have to tell you is going to break your heart. There was a newspaper clipping tucked into the book. It's the death notice for Stanley Morgan, August 3rd, 1983. It gives only his mother and father as surviving relatives – Margaret Ann Lashley Morgan and John Percy Morgan."

"Oh God, Kev, how did he die?"

"This only says his death was on August second and was unexpected."

"In the photographs I've seen him growing up. He was a cute kid, who grew into a very handsome man. Interesting, though – he never married. Among all these pictures, there aren't any of him with a woman. I still have more to look through."

"I'm sorry to have had to tell you about the death notice over the phone, but I didn't want to wait until I got home."

"That is so sad, even though we suspected that something must have happened to him. Still, it's tragic that he died so young."

"Yeah," Kevin responded. "He was only forty-two. His father lived sixteen years after losing his son, and poor Margaret lived nine years feeling the loss of both her husband and her boy. Add to that, Margaret now seems isolated, and she desperately wants to join them."

Chapter **Four**

"I'll try to finish the sorting today," Cathy told Kevin on the phone. "I had hoped to read the diary while you were at work, but I got caught up in these photos and don't want to stop now." Cathy paused for a moment. "I need to go out tomorrow to get some milk and stuff, but first I'll drive to the newspaper office in Bedford. Maybe there's a way to search Stanley's name, and maybe we can come up with something more than just his death notice."

"That's a great idea about checking newspaper records."

"It wasn't my idea, Kev, it was Margaret's. I heard a thump at the front door and when I opened it, I saw that someone had thrown a rolled up newspaper against it. Since we didn't subscribe to the paper, I figured our friendly ghost Margaret must have delivered it."

"And you got the message. Good for you, Cathy. If you don't hear from me, you'll know there's nothing new here at Margaret's house."

After hanging up, Kevin helped Bill carry a cedar chest down the steps and out into the van. As they wrapped it in padding, he told a fib. "I'm going to keep that baby book that was under the dresser. I know the son's girlfriend, and I think she'd like to have it."

Bill shrugged. "Keep whatever you want. It makes no difference to me."

* * * * *

The remainder of the loading proved uneventful. Kevin drove back to his home, where Bill had left his car. Parking the loaded van in his drive, he said goodbye to his coworker and went inside. It was after six and he was hungry.

"Did you unload everything already?"

"No. There was just too much. We'll do it tomorrow, hon. Now, I need to spend this evening with you – and I'm starved."

"Good, because I have pork chops and baked potatoes that are about done, so by the time you've changed your clothes and washed up, I'll have a salad made, and we'll be all set to eat. We can talk photographs and stuff after dinner."

The unsolved mystery of why Margaret's spiritual entity had been unable to escape was too compelling. Halfway through his chop, Kevin laid down his fork and said, "Isn't it amazing how that baby book matched the book in your dream?"

Cathy put her fork down also and responded, "And what is even more amazing is that it cried, because that record of his beginning also held the record of his end."

"But not the why," Kevin stated. "It only gave us the date, and not the cause of Stanley's death. What the hell does 'unexpected' mean? Did he look at all sickly or disabled in the later photographs?"

"No, he looked pretty healthy to me, and as I said, he was a good-looking man."

"But he never married. Strange." Kevin pushed his plate back and concentrated on finishing his glass of milk.

"I was thinking that maybe he was married, but somewhere along the way there was a nasty divorce, and all the pictures of his ex-wife were thrown away."

Kevin stood. "I'm wrapping up the rest of my chop and potato. I can warm it up later. You go ahead and finish I want to look at those pictures that were taken around 1983."

"I've lost my appetite, too. There's just too much going through my head, so while you're looking at the pictures, I'll check the diary entries made in the fall of '83."

After wrapping up their leftovers, each took a cup of coffee, Kevin to the kitchen table and Cathy into the living room. She had sorted all the dated pictures into chronological order, and Kevin started looking at those dated 1982. He was curious, however, and so he looked back at pictures of Stanley in his childhood. "That was a great looking family," he called out to his wife, but she was absorbed in reading and did not respond. A cold breeze, however, blew across the back of his neck and he knew Margaret had heard him.

In the 1982 batch of photos, Kevin noted several of Stan and one or two other men. While reaching for his coffee, he knocked over the 1970 pile. As he restacked them, he noticed more pictures of Margaret's son with other men. "What are you telling me, Margaret? What is it you want me to know about Stan?"

Just then Cathy called out, "Kevin, here's a clue." Before he had time to answer, she headed into the kitchen. "I was going to focus in on what Margaret wrote in the early '80s, but first I skimmed some of the earlier entries. Listen to this one. It's dated February ninth, back in 1965.

John and I had a long heart-to-heart talk with Stan tonight. He told us what we already suspected, and we reassured him that he was our son and we loved him no matter what. I must admit that I cried for an hour after our talk, and this is the hardest entry I have had to make since learning that I could only have one child."

"So, what was it he told her?" Kevin wondered out loud.

"She doesn't say in the diary – at least, not in the following dozen or so pages. I wonder if he had a terminal illness?"

"Did you notice all the pictures of Stan with other men?" Pausing, Kevin held one up of Stan standing with a man who appeared to be ten years younger. "Like this one."

"Are you thinking what I'm thinking?" Cathy asked.

"Probably. I'm thinking that Stanley was gay."

"I wonder if he died of AIDS? I think by 1983 cases were showing up."

Just then the toilet began to flush in the bathroom. "Buster?" Cathy asked.

"Margaret," Kevin stated as he ran into to where the toilet was still flushing. "You've got to see this, Cathy. The vortex is spinning counter-clockwise!"

"So?"

"North of the Equator it should only spin clockwise. This is going in the wrong direction. My God, Cathy, what if *we're* going in the wrong direction?"

"So maybe Stan wasn't gay?"

"But the toilet didn't flush until we speculated that he died of AIDS. I think he probably was gay, but maybe it wasn't AIDS that killed him."

"The mystery continues," Cathy said holding the diary in her hands. "Oh, Margaret, what secrets must we still learn? What more do you need to tell us?"

"Tomorrow, you concentrate on the diary. I need to go downtown, so we can get the truck unloaded, but then *I'll* head up to the newspaper office in Bedford and see what I can learn. That'll save you the trip. Besides, the warehouse is closer to Bedford than the grocery store."

Cathy nodded her acceptance of the change in plans. "I baked a frozen cherry pie for dinner. It might still be warm. Would you like a slice with some ice cream?"

"Sounds good to me. Let's see if we can catch some news. We've got to refocus on the living. The Morgan family secrets can wait until tomorrow."

* * * * *

After a good night's sleep, Kevin and Cathy devoured a sausage and pancake breakfast, given that both spouses were hungry due to their having cut short the prior night's dinner. "You don't have to unload alone, do you?" Cathy asked after wiping away the maple syrup that had dripped down her chin.

"No. Bill will be there to help, plus some of the guys that work in the warehouse. It should go quickly."

"And you'll go to the newspaper office in Bedford to see if you can come up with something?"

"Yep. Right after the truck is emptied, I'll head up there, and if there's time, I want to check the house out once more, before I turn in the key." Kevin added more syrup to his half-eaten stack of pancakes. As he set the syrup pitcher on the table, he spilled a glob. "Look at this, Cathy. The syrup has formed an X. Is Margaret referring to something explicit, or wanting us to X something out?"

Cathy got up to look. "It seems to be changing. Look! Now it resembles a pair of scissors!"

"What does she want us to cut out?"

"I think we're going to have to wait, Kevin. There are probably a lot more pieces to this puzzle."

"The glob changed when you looked at it, Cathy. I wonder if that has any significance."

"You know how girls connect," Cathy said as she dipped her finger into the spilled maple syrup, and then brought it to her mouth. She licked and grinned.

"You're so naughty."

"Isn't that why you married me?" She planted a syrupy, open-mouthed kiss on Kevin's lips. "Call me today when you get a chance, big boy."

"I've got to run, but I'll call from the newspaper office and let you know what I found out."

Keep your cell on, and I'll call you if I find anything new in the diary," Cathy promised."

They exchanged one more syrupy kiss.

* * * * *

Bill was waiting at the warehouse when Kevin arrived. "I'm getting old, Kev. I was sore last night. How'd you sleep?"

"Cathy and I have been trying to deal with a…a mystery of sorts. It's consumed a lot of time and energy."

"Well, let me know if I can help in any way."

"Thanks, Bill. You can begin by helping me get that furniture out of the back of the van."

The pair got the van emptied by noon. After a quick lunch, Kevin drove to the newspaper's office in Bedford, where he parked in an area reserved for trucks. He walked through the front entrance into a larger room with a counter separating a small waiting area from a workspace containing three desks. Of the women working at desks, only one looked up and prepared to rise out of her chair, but her phone rang. Another woman motioned the third woman in Kevin's direction. That one, the youngest of the three, came to the counter.

"How can I help you, sir?"

"I'm looking for some information on a man who died in 1983. The paper ran his death notice, and I hoped that there might have been a story about the man's life or his death. I can give you his name, and the names of his mother and father, if that would help."

"What was the date?" Having pushed her bangs out of her eyes, she picked up a pencil from the counter.

"The death notice was in the August third edition, but it said he died on August second, in 1983."

"Oh, 1983. Why, that's over 20 years ago. We don't keep papers that long, and we only got computerized about fifteen years ago. Sorry, but I can't help."

Kevin was about to leave when the older woman who had been on the phone came to the counter. She looked at the younger woman. "Are things under control here?"

"He's looking for papers from August, back in 1983. I told him we don't have any copies that old, and that was before we started storing them on computer discs."

"Oh, before you came to work here, Becky, we took our archive of old issues to the public library. We were running out of space." This older woman turned to Kevin. "If you ask at the library's reference desk, they should be able to help you."

Having thanked the two ladies, Kevin headed for the library. On his way he called Cathy. "Hi, hon. There's nothing at the newspaper office that old, but I was told that the issues from the eighties are stored at the library. I'm on my way there now."

"Well, all I've come up with so far is the first name Steven. This man's referred to in the diary as Stan's friend, but could be his lover, and it was in '83. The next thing for me to do is look again at pictures, to see if I can find a picture of this guy Steve."

"I guess we'll both be busy, then. I'll be back in touch."

As he approached the library, he looked for a place to park. He finally had to settle for parking in an area with a sign stating No Trucks, but he had no other option. Once inside, he headed for the reference desk: an actual desk separate from the counter that handled circulation. He stood waiting for a full ten minutes before a matronly woman emerged from the rows of shelves just off to his left.

"How can I help?" she asked, peering over the top of her reading glasses that had slid halfway down her nose.

"I'm looking for old local newspapers dating back to August, and maybe even July, 1983."

"I can't promise every issue, but what we have would be stored in the basement. I have to stay up here, but I think things are pretty well organized down there, so you'll have no problem finding what you want. Of course, you can't check anything out from the archives, but we can make photocopies of articles for you – at twenty-five cents a copy, that is."

"That's great. How do I get there?"

"Follow me. The door to the basement is locked, so I'll have to open it for you. Then you're on your own."

Kevin followed the librarian, who waddled a bit as she walked. Once she unlocked and opened the basement door, she reached through it and flipped the light switch. Dim lights came on.

"How will I be able to see down there?"

"Don't worry. There are a lot of hanging lights – just pull their chain. You'll see that there are also a few tables, each with a bright desk lamp, so you'll do just fine."

Kevin thanked her and headed down the steps. When he reached the bottom, he heard the door at the top close. The librarian had apparently watched to be sure that he didn't trip and fall. Once down, Kevin became aware of the sound of dehumidifiers emitting a constant white noise that would not interfere with his thinking. He tried his cell phone, but it searched for a signal without success. Ahead he saw a sign that simply stated NEWSPAPERS. An arrow directed him to turn left at the end of a row of shelves filled with labeled boxes.

On making the turn, he saw more shelves, but these had been identified by a sign stating Bedford Daily News. Off to the right he spied a long table with four chairs and two gooseneck desk lamps. He was thankful for the pads of paper and pencils on the table, for he had failed to bring anything to write on or write with. On closer inspection of the boxes stacked on the shelves, he discovered that each was clearly labeled. *This is going to be easy*, he thought when he realized that the contents of each box were identified by month and year. Standing on a stepstool, he reached up to the top shelf and pulled out the July 1983 box. After carrying it to the table, he returned to retrieve that year's August issues.

First, he looked through the papers from the first to the fourth day in August, but found only the August third death notice. He then perused the issues, beginning from the end of July and working foreward. At the bottom of the front page of the July twenty-eighth edition, Kevin's attention was drawn to the headline *Stabbing Victim Remains Critical*. In the body of the article he read silently of Stanley Morgan's failure to regain consciousness following his stabbing on the evening of July twenty-sixth. Kevin quickly found and read the lead front page story of the July twenty-seventh issue.

Last night, Stanley Morgan, age forty-two and lifelong resident of Bedford, was found stabbed and bleeding in the alley between Market and High Streets. He is reported to have been unconscious and to have remained so throughout the night. Hospital officials describe his condition as critical. Police sources state that the victim received multiple stab wounds, but no weapon was found, and there were no witnesses to the attack. The reason for the assault was unknown, but robbery was ruled out, as Mr. Morgan still had his watch and wallet. The investigation led by Detective Michael Miller continues.

"Ah, damn," Kevin said out loud. "This makes me sick to my stomach." The cold breeze was hardly noticeable in the cool basement, but the blinking of the lamp was a clear indication that Margaret had heard him. "Yes, Margaret, I now understand your pain." Having jotted down the lead detective's name, he then went back to the early August issues.

In the August sixth issue he read: *The murder of Stanley Morgan, the forty-two-year-old stabbing victim who died on August second from wounds inflicted on July twenty-sixth, remains under investigation. The victim never regained consciousness, and no witnesses have come forward. Detective Michael Miller said that the knife used in the stabbing has not been found, and added that there were no clues as to the identity of the assailant. Anyone with information is urged to contact the Bedford Police Department.*

As Kevin searched the following papers, he found additional discouraging news of the lack of evidence and the failure to identify any suspects. The reports became shorter, and soon were no longer front page news. By mid-September, the newspaper had forgotten the story, and Kevin assumed that the police had also. He wouldn't forget, however, and his next stop was going to be the police department.

Chapter Five

In the archives of the library, Kevin learned of Stanley's unsolved murder. Emerging from the library basement, he went to the reference desk where the librarian was sorting papers. "I finished downstairs, and I've turned off the lights," he informed her.

She looked up from her work, her glasses now hanging on a chain around her neck. "Do you need anything copied?"

"No, thanks. I jotted down all the information I need." He turned to leave, but stopped and turned back. "How do I get to the police station from here?"

She pointed. "Go out the front door and turn left. Take another left on Hudson, and you can't miss it. You'll see it on your right. But, it's within walking distance."

Kevin thanked her, but decided to drive. When he got to his truck, he spotted a yellow piece of paper stuck under the driver's side windshield wiper. "Damn," he muttered out loud. "I got a ticket." To himself he added, *Well, I was going to the station anyway*.

However, when he plucked the paper from beneath the wiper, he discovered that it was a promotional ad for an art exhibit being held in a local gallery. He contemplated dropping it on the ground, but he figured he got by with parking illegally, so he'd better not get fined for littering. Having stuck it in his shirt pocket, he climbed into the cab of his truck.

Once inside, he called Cathy. "Hi, hon," he said before giving her the bad news. "I have more information that's hard to hear. It's worse than we've suspected. Stan was murdered. He was stabbed repeatedly and left to die in an alley. He was unconscious in the hospital for days before passing away."

"Oh, my God. This breaks my heart. Who did it? Who killed him?"

"That's what makes the story even worse. The murderer was apparently never found. There seems to be no summary or conclusion in the papers."

"Oh, his poor mother and dad. What a tragedy, and for the murder to go unsolved! Will you be coming home now?"

"I wish I could, but not yet, hon. I have to go to the police station and talk with the detective who had been on the case. Have you found anything new?"

"Just several pictures of Stan and Steve in the pile of unmarked photos. I'm eager to show them to you and get your opinion. It looks as if they span several years."

"Cathy, I'm not ready to quit for the day. I'm leaving the library now and, like I said, I'm going to the police station to talk with Detective Miller. He's the one the newspaper articles cited as leading the murder investigation. I've got to talk with him."

"This might be women's intuition, Kev, but I have the strong feeling that this unsolved murder is somehow the key to setting Margaret free. If her only son was killed and someone got away with it, my hunch is that she needs us to find the one who killed him. Then she'd finally be free to join her husband and son."

"I think you might be right, hon, and I'm hoping this detective can give us a good start on solving the mystery."

"Good luck. Apparently that detective didn't have any."

After saying goodbye, Kevin drove the short distance to the police station. After parking in a truck-friendly spot, he walked into the station and up to the front desk where a young officer sat reading a magazine. "I'd like to talk with Detective Miller."

"Who?" the officer asked.

"Michael Miller. Detective Michael Miller."

"Never heard of him."

"But the newspaper said he was the lead detective on a murder case back in 1983."

"We're talking a quarter of a century, then. Hang on – I'll have to get one of the older officers up here. Maybe he'll remember this guy, if he's even still alive."

The young uniformed officer lifted his phone and punched in an extension number. "Detective Johnston, there's a fellow up here asking about a Detective Miller who was here in the eighties." The officer was silent for a minute. "Yeah, that's it, Michael Miller." There was another brief period while the officer listened. He then looked back at Kevin. "Detective Johnston said he'll be out in a couple minutes. Have a seat over there." He pointed to the line of wooden chairs against the wall.

After a five minute delay, a man in plainclothes who appeared to be in his sixties came out of an office and motioned to Kevin. "Come on back. We'll talk." Kevin followed him into the office. "Close the door and sit down. I'm Detective Johnston, and you are?"

"Kevin. Kevin Riley."

"I haven't seen you around, Kevin. Are you from here?"

"No, my wife and I live in Cruxton, and we both grew up there."

"Well, what brings you to Bedford looking for Detective Miller?"

Kevin had not expected that question. He didn't feel as if he could start talking about the nineteen-year-old spirit of a ninety-year-old dead woman. He had to make up a story quickly. "I've enrolled in the adult education classes back at the Cruxton Community College, and my focus is on becoming a crime reporter for a newspaper. The professor came up with a cold case for me to research, and I started with the Bedford newspapers archived in the library basement."

"And you came up with the name Michael Miller?"

"Yeah. The article in August of 1983 said he was the lead investigator of a murder, but I couldn't find any report of it ever being solved."

"What was the case?"

"A fellow named Morgan – Stanley Morgan – was found dying in an alley somewhere here in town. The guy finally died, never having regaining consciousness. According to the newspaper accounts, no clues to his murderer were ever found."

"Wait. Was that the case of the gay guy who was shot?"

"Stabbed. He was stabbed."

"Yeah, I remember the case. I was pretty new on the force, so when the guy was found, my job was to scour the alley looking for the weapon. I never did find it."

"Since Miller is no longer here, do you think I could read his report?"

"You know, that should be public knowledge, but given the trouble we'd have to go to in order to find the report, I think I'll just send you off to talk with Mike."

"So he's still alive. Good. Where will I find him?"

"I'll give you his phone number," the detective glanced at his watch, "but just about now I'll bet you'll find him at the Rainbow Coffee Shop across the street and down a block. He goes there just about every day to flirt with a redheaded waitress he's been flirting with for the past twenty-some years. He was been no more successful in snagging her than he was in solving crimes. Just look for a bald guy with a big belly, and I'll bet he's wearing a T-shirt."

Kevin thanked him and walked out. His first impulse was to jaywalk, but he thought it best to walk up to the corner, where he crossed and proceeded down the other side.

The coffee shop was small. Three slender men with full heads of hair sat on stools at the counter. Three round tables in the middle of the room stood empty, and two elderly women sat at the fourth. Booths lined the wall next to the window. Sitting in one was a bald man with a big belly. Even without his T-shirt, he would have been easy to spot. Kevin first bought himself a cup of the house coffee at the counter, added a little cream, and then cautiously approached the booth where the man sat.

"Detective Miller?"

The man looked up. "Mike. Just Mike Miller now. What can I do for you, young man?"

"If you're not busy, I'd like to sit with you and talk about an unsolved case you were on about twenty-five years ago."

"The Morgan case?"

"How'd you guess?"

"Not a day has gone by that I've not mourned the fact that I could never crack that case. Long after I was told to drop it, that man's mother and father would come to me looking for closure. Their son had been killed, and it was my job to find the killer, but I never could. That haunts me to this day."

"Can I sit?"

"Yes, join me." Mike gestured toward the seat across the table. "Sit."

Kevin slid into the booth. "I've heard you come here often."

"I started coming here when I first started on that case. I needed someplace where I could soak up some decent coffee and think. Eventually I noticed the waitress, who back then had an shape that would cause a blind man's heart to skip a beat, but that's another of my failure stories. So, young fellow, tell me about your interest in the Morgan case."

Kevin thought of his community college story, but decided to be upfront with Mike. "You might not believe this, but if you think you've been haunted, let me tell you of our experience." He then proceeded to tell of the semi-transparent apparition seen by both him and his wife, of Margaret's way of giving them information and a sense of direction, and of how they believed she was stuck because she still needed closure on the case of her son's murder..

Kevin felt sure that the retired detective thought he must surely be insane, but instead Mike took a deep breath and said, "I've seen her, too. I didn't dare tell anyone, but she appeared about six months ago."

"That was probably around the time she died," Kevin observed.

"I'm sorry to learn she's gone, but that's what I figured. She must have been pretty old."

"I think she was ninety when she passed away. Her husband John had died eight or nine years before her."

"I would see that faint image of the mother at a young age, but she was crying and I knew they were the same tears she had cried when her son was taken away and I couldn't find the one who robbed him of his life. During her last visit just a few days ago, I also heard young children singing, and I've been watching for that choir."

"How about the choir leader – the music teacher? My wife is an elementary school music teacher. I think Margaret might have been telling you that we were coming."

Mike slid to the edge of his chair. "Then tell me how I can help."

"Let's start with anything you learned that wasn't in the newspaper reports."

"Well, by now you probably know that Stanley was homosexual."

"Yes, and we think he might have been having a relationship with a younger man named Steven. Does that name ring a bell?"

"I did interview a man by that name – an artist who had been rumored to be in a relationship with Stanley – but Steven claimed it was just a good friendship. I also remember that he had an airtight alibi for the night of the murder. He was displaying his paintings at a local gallery and was seen there by a number of reputable people."

Kevin reached into his shirt pocket for the yellow slip of paper that had been tucked under his wiper blade, but the pocket was empty.

Mike hesitated, looked down and shook his head. "I would have continued to look for evidence and pursue leads, but then Chief Bailey pulled me off the case, saying it was probably just a hate crime and was a waste of the department's time."

"And that was it? The case was closed?"

"Yes, officially, that was it. Unofficially, I still snooped around, but I kept bumping into brick walls. Nobody wanted to talk to me, and I felt powerless. I felt I had let his mom and dad down."

"This almost smacks of prejudice. The department was quick to write it off because the victim was gay."

"You said it, and that started at the top."

Suddenly a vintage jukebox in the corner lit up and started playing, but after only a couple of lines from a fifties recording by Fats Domino, "Ain't that a shame, my tears fell like rain..." Suddenly, the machine stopped and went dark.

The waitress ran out of the kitchen. "Was that the jukebox? It hasn't worked in years!" She looked behind it. "Hey, the damn thing isn't even plugged in!"

Kevin observed that she did not have the figure she must have had twenty years earlier.

"Spooky," Mike said. "Better let me hold you."

"You're the spooky one, Michael," the waitress said as she walked back into the kitchen.

"Phew, if she hadn't come out," Kevin confessed, "I would have burst into tears."

"Me too," Mike said as a single drop ran down his cheek.

"I think Margaret knows that the police gave up on her son because he was gay."

"Ain't it a shame." At that point the old detective's eyes filled up. "I failed," he managed to say before he began to sob. "I should have stood up to Chief Bailey."

That was all it took. Kevin began openly to cry also, and the two men stood and held each other.

"Now this takes the cake. Two grown men crying." The voice was that of the waitress. Neither man noticed that she'd come out of the kitchen.

"Back off, lady," Mike barked angrily at the waitress.

"Yes, sir, Master Mike. Oh, Daddy, where have you been hiding? The dominant detective finally figured out how to turn me on. I've been bad such a bad girl, so handcuff me."

"Let's get out of here," Michael said, laying a five dollar bill on the table. "Here's a tip," he said to the waitress. "Grow up." He led the way out of the shop, with Kevin following and the waitress standing with her mouth hanging open.

"I'd like you to meet with Cathy, my wife," Kevin said, adding with a wink, "as long as you're nice."

With a wink back, the old cop said, "I've been nice to that waitress for over twenty years and never got to first base."

"Dinner tonight or lunch tomorrow. Your choice."

"Is your wife a good cook?"

"That she is, so is it dinner tonight?"

"Yeah. I'm parked outside. I'll follow you, if you're ready to go now."

"I was going to swing by the empty Morgan house, but that can wait. Tell me this, though, is the art gallery here in town still open?"

"No, that place closed about eight years ago. It's an auto parts store now."

Kevin found that the yellow piece of paper had reappeared in his pocket. He unfolded it, but it was blank. He stuck it back in his pocket and turned to Mike. "I'm parked at the back of the lot – the moving van. Follow me." As he walked to his truck, he phoned Cathy. "Plan on having a dinner guest. Detective Miller, the original investigator on the case, is coming home with me. Margaret has visited him also, and she told him about you."

"Really? She told him about me?"

"You know, the girl connection? But seriously, she did it in her clever, cryptic way. So, can you handle two hungry men?"

"Oh, Kevin, you know that's been a favorite fantasy of mine."

"You're so naughty. We'll be there by 6:30."

"We'll have chicken, mashed potatoes with gravy, buttered limas and cornbread muffins."

"He'll be surprised. I told him you were a lousy cook."

"Then you'll both have to go hungry."

"'Ain't that a shame?'"

"Where'd that come from?"

"It's in an old song."

"I know, but what made you think of it right now?"

"Oh, it just popped into my head."

"Spooky, but I suspect Margaret has communicated with you again."

* * * * *

Cathy met Kevin and Michael at the door. "You must be the infamous detective I've heard so much about." She extended her hand.

Mike took her hand gently in his. "And you must be Cathy. Your husband didn't tell me how beautiful you are."

"He only married me because I'm a good cook."

"So I've heard, but also a grade school...ah, I mean, elementary school music teacher."

Cathy looked at her husband. "How did that come up?"

"That's how Margaret told him you'd be coming into his life. She arranged for a heavenly children's choir to sing for him."

"I'm sure she figured that you'd be tagging along right behind me, Kev," Cathy said, getting her first kiss from him since he walked in the door. "Welcome home."

"I think Margaret figured I'd be tagging along, too, so does that mean I get a kiss too?" Mike joked.

Cathy kissed him on the top of his bald head, and then rubbed it. "It feels like my husband's bare bottom."

"Impossible," Kevin protested. "My bottom is hairier."

"But his head's prettier. Now let's get serious," Cathy urged.

"About solving a case?" her husband asked.

"No, about eating dinner, and be sure to save room for some warm apple pie."

As they sat around the dining room table, despite the good food eliciting rave reviews, they found time to talk of the prejudicial treatment of the case back in 1983. "Things have changed," Mike stressed. "The old Chief is in a mental institution, and the sergeant who supported him is dead. The new brass, Chief Harris, is quite tolerant, and one of the officers is openly gay and accepted by all."

"Can the case be reopened?" Cathy asked, and then passed the gravy boat to the retired detective who had just helped himself to another mound of mashed potatoes. "Be sure to save room for dessert," she reminded him.

Mike patted his belly. "I've got plenty of room in here. As far as opening up cold cases, it's not as easy as it is on TV."

"Would it help if we came up with some new evidence?" Kevin asked.

"Yes, that would definitely help, but without something new, the case is closed."

"Then we'll find new evidence," Cathy said, "but where do we start?"

"With one more helping of limas," Mike said. "Would you pass them to me, please?"

Chapter Six

Mike, the retired detective who had been taken off the case of Stanley's murder, finished his dinner and sat back in his chair. "Thank you, Mrs. Riley. That was delicious." He then got up and picked up a stack of dirty plates. Walking into the kitchen, he nodded toward the stacks of pictures on the kitchen table. "Family photos?"

"Kevin didn't tell you about these, then?" Cathy asked. "These are the Morgan family photos. I've been getting them in chronological order. I'll tell you about some of them, once we get the dining room cleaned up." She had already put the pots and pans into the dishwasher, so with the three of them working together, the cleanup didn't take long.

Kevin pushed the start button on the washer and announced, "Done. Let's look at pictures and talk."

The three sat at the kitchen table. One photo stuck out from a stack of pictures lying face down. Mike plucked it out, first reading the date on the back: "July fourth, 1983. That was the month Stanley was murdered." Having turned the photo over, he remained silent for a minute. "It's the three of them – mother, father and son. It's the way I remember the parents," Mike commented, "but I never saw this young man alive." He wiped away a tear.

"Look at these pictures. They are also within the last few month of Stan's life, but in these he's with the young man we think was his lover." She handed the stack to Mike who studied each one of them.

"That's the Steve we talked of in the coffee shop," Kevin added. "He's the artist who you said had an alibi for the night of the stabbing."

"But this is not the Steve I interviewed."

"What?"

"This is not the Steve I interviewed," he repeated. "The Steve I interviewed, the artist, was black." He looked at the back of the photos. "Yeah, the name Steve is written on some of these, but this must be a different one. Definitely not the Steven I inter-viewed who claimed to be Steve's friend."

"Okay, gang. I think Margaret told me to let go of the artist Steve, wanted me to be aware that there were two men with the same first name." He pulled the yellow piece of paper out of his shirt pocket and opened it. "The paper is blank, but when I first read it, it was an announcement about an art exhibit at a gallery that Mike says has been closed for years. I should have looked at the date and at the artist's name, but as soon as I saw it wasn't a parking ticket I stuck it in my pocket."

"But, the name Steve is on the back of photos, and it also comes up in Margaret's diary. The dates of entries mentioning him go back years."

"Then the white Steve, not the artist, seen in the photos and mentioned in the diary must be an ex-lover, and a long-term one at that," Kevin stated.

"X," exclaimed Cathy. "The syrup X we saw this morning."

Mike seemed bewildered, so they told of the drop from the syrup pitcher that formed an X and then transformed itself into a pair of scissors.

"Yes," Kevin exclaimed, "Margaret seems not to be telling us to cross something off, but to find this ex-lover."

"You think he's the killer?" Cathy asked.

"If he is," Mike stated, "a drop of syrup is not the kind of evidence that would hold up in court."

"And why did it turn into what looked like scissors?" Cathy asked.

"I think this is going to prove more complicated, and the ex-Steve is just another piece in a very complex puzzle. Tomorrow I have to go back to the house," Kevin said. "I want to be sure we didn't miss anything."

"I've been distracted by sorting these pictures, but tomorrow I'm going to start over and read Margaret's diary from beginning to end." She looked again at a picture of a small boy wearing corduroy kickers, standing between his mother and dad. "What a shame."

"And I'm going to the station to look at the case file, just on the chance I've missed something. Even though I'm now retired, they'll give me access to the files. I'll also check to see if there were any gay-bashing reports during that period."

Buster, who had been curled up under the table, meowed. "He's reminding us that he's part of the team," Cathy noted, adding "Let's plan to have dinner here tomorrow and compare notes."

"No need to cook for us again," Mike said. "I'll pick up a couple of pizzas on my way into town."

"And I'll get the beer," Kevin offered.

The hanging light over the table flickered. Everyone smiled. Margaret Morgan was excited.

* * * * *

After Mike left, Kevin and Cathy talked about the former detective and the role he might play in solving the cold case of Stanley's murder. "He might just be another contact that Margaret can communicate through. "I think having seen how hearing children singing formed the prediction that he'd meet you, and after the unplugged jukebox played 'Ain't it a Shame,'" he'll recognize any new messages from her."

Cathy suggested that Mike's role could be working with the police to get a new investigation started. "He's probably got some good connections, and as he said, the attitude of the department has changed, in terms of accepting diversity."

Once in bed they drifted off to sleep without having set the alarm. Kevin woke, however, when the automatic coffeemaker began to gurgle: the first sounds made when it started its preprogrammed early morning task. Cathy also began to stir. "You awake?" he whispered.

"Yeah, that coffee pot seems unusually loud this morning."

"A message from Margaret?"

"No, I think we're just used to getting up at this time. Even without the alarm our mental clocks probably woke us."

"Well, I'm ready to get a start on this day," Kevin announced as he rolled out of bed. "If you're getting up, I'll bring you your coffee."

Cathy went into the bathroom to begin her morning shower, but before stepping into it, she heard her husband call her name. "What, hon?"

"Did you leave the iron on last night?"

"No, I left it on the kitchen counter, but it was unplugged. I wanted to add some water so I could steam-press a pair of my slacks."

"Well, it's hot. But wait, it's not plugged in."

Cathy walked into the kitchen. "Hot?" she asked.

"She's sent us another message. It's something about hot, or iron, or ironing."

"Or steam, or maybe slacks."

"It's probably just another small piece of the puzzle that will fit in somewhere."

"I sure wish that ghosts were issued cell phones. That would make things a lot easier."

Just then Kevin's cell phone chimed its notice of an incoming call. Startled, Cathy and Kevin looked at each other. "My God," Cathy said, "she's calling us."

Kevin hesitated, but the phone persisted. Reluctantly he answered it with a meek "Hello."

"Kevin, it's Mike. I was thinking, when you come to Bedford today, bring a picture of that unidentified Steve, the one you think was Stanley's intimate friend. I'll check it against the mug shots down at the station."

"I'll be there about 9:30 this morning."

"Great. I'll meet you at the Morgan house."

After hanging up, Cathy stated, "I had another dream last night." She poured herself a cup of coffee.

"Message?"

"No, massage?"

"What?"

"Some gorgeous young man in a police uniform gave me a full body massage, and I do mean full body."

"So, my naughty wife was seducing a cop."

"Actually, it was a really lousy massage. I kept telling him he was doing it all wrong, and he kept telling me he was just a beginner."

"I'm starting to keep notes on all the little pieces that might fit somewhere in the puzzle, but I think sometimes Margaret throws something in just to tease us. I'm going to add this dream, but with a question mark. Maybe your hormones were just acting up last night."

"Had it been my hormones, that cop would have done a better job."

"You're downright nasty, woman."

"I do have the feeling this was intended to be more playful than serious, and I think Margaret was the dream's author."

"And then she also would have picked the costumes. Are there any other details you remember?"

"Yes, now that I think about it. I noticed that the cop's holster was empty. When I asked him about it, he told me that his gun didn't work."

"Hmmm. Do we have an impotent cop here? I'm wondering if it was a dream about Mike's feelings of helplessness. He wanted to continue the investigation of Stanley's murder, but felt impotent and let Former Chief Bailey's prejudices against gays win out over justice."

"That's not really helpful, because we already knew that," Cathy said, "but we need to be writing all of this stuff down anyway. Our first interpretation might not always be accurate."

"That reminds me, Cathy. See if you can find out what kind of work Stan did. Margaret might have mentioned it in her diary. I'll also ask Mike to check the case file since it might be mentioned there."

* * * * *

By 8:45 Kevin had showered, dressed, eaten breakfast and said goodbye to Cathy. He pulled into the driveway of Margaret's home at 9:20. The detective was sitting on the porch steps, awaiting him.

"Morning, Mike," said Kevin. "I brought three pictures with that Steve, all dated 1982."

"Good. I'm going now to the station, and I'll see if he matches any mug shots in the ten years around that date. Even for a small town, that'll be quite a few, but mostly drunk and disorderly charges. I'll be in touch, Mr. Riley. You let me know if you discover anything of significance."

"I really don't expect to find anything new in the house. We cleaned it out pretty well, but I'll feel better if I look around one more time."

Sounding like a detective, Mike advised, "Be sure to check around the outside also, and if you see cans of garbage or trash, look through those. You never know."

Mike had turned to leave when Kevin remembered the question striking Cathy and himself. "See if the case file tells what kind of work Stanley did."

"I don't need to check the file. I remember. He was a door-to-door salesman."

"He wasn't selling scissors or irons, was he?"

"No, vacuum sweepers."

"Darn, that doesn't fit."

"If the case had been easy, Kevin, I would've solved it a quarter of a century ago." He waved goodbye, got in his car and drove off.

Kevin walked the length of the long front porch before entering the house. It occurred to him to look under the porch as well, and he had thought to bring a flashlight, knowing that the electricity had been turned off in the house. Since portions of the latticework were broken, he peered through these openings. There was nothing suspicious.

Once in the house, he walked through the parlor, living room and dining room, but nothing remained. The kitchen had also been stripped of everything moveable. As he opened the back door, he saw what he guessed to be the same squirrel he had seen before. The critter was sitting upright with its tail curled behind its back, looking
straight at Kevin. Kevin hesitated before opening the screen door, and when he did, the squirrel turned, leaped onto the top of a metal trash can and then onto the ground.

Kevin went immediately to that can, expecting it to be filled with rotting garbage. When he pulled off the lid, he was relieved to find that it contained birdseed. A plastic scoop rested on top of the seed. Scooping up a full load, he spread it around the platform feeder. After he replaced the lid, he had a second thought. Removing the lid again, he dug his hands down into the seed. Nothing.

I guess Mr. Squirrel wasn't telling me what Margaret wanted. He was telling me what he wanted. The poor critter was hungry. Kevin spread another scoopful of seed on the ground around the post supporting the feeder. Two other cans behind the house proved to be empty. One still smelled of garbage.

Kevin moved his search to the second floor. Closets in the bed rooms all received a thorough inspection, but nothing new turned up. The bathroom was bare. He directed his attention to the tower room. On entering the empty room, he noticed something he had not noticed before. The house was obviously heated by hot water. In every other room there were old-fashioned standing iron radiators. In the tower room, the radiator had been covered on all sides. Kevin knew that one of the reasons, beyond aesthetics, was to keep heat from being absorbed by the outside wall behind it. That meant there was a space between the cover and the wall.

The words *iron* and *hot* reverberated in his mind as he looked behind the first radiator cover, but saw nothing but cobwebs. However, behind the second one, something that looked like a ledger came in view. He couldn't quite reach it with his hand, and so he returned to his truck to retrieve a broom. He was able to poke the ledger with the handle until it slid out the other side. He could tell that the ledger was old, and that caused him to worry that the pages might have dried and become brittle over the years. To his delight, he found that everything inside was in good shape.

The book appeared to be Stanley's record of his sales route, listing the stops he had made when peddling the vacuum sweepers. On a closer inspection, Kevin noted that the ledger covered the years from 1981 and into the first six months of 1983. He also noted that the entries were for businesses only, not for individual households.

Kevin hit the speed dial and Cathy answered the phone. "Cathy, I just made an interesting find, although I'm still not sure what pertinent information it might provide. Stanley was a salesman who sold vacuum sweepers door to door, but also to businesses. I found his ledger, showing the dates and names of the business he dealt with. It must have been on top of a radiator cover and got knocked off. It fell behind the cover, and had it not been for Margaret's hot clue I might not have looked there."

Cathy also had something to report. "Oh, good! I've also discovered something that might or might not be significant. On May thirteenth of 1983, Margaret made an entry about things coming apart at the stitches for Stanley. A few pages later she wrote of the pain caused when things come unstitched. It's all very cryptic."

"Bookmark those pages."

"Already done! Plus, there's an earlier short note, simply stating that she and John had met J – just the initial J – and that could be one of their friends, or a woman, or...well...who knows? But I marked the page, anyway."

"I haven't heard anything more from Mike. I'm about to head for home, but he's got my cell phone number, and he knows he's invited for dinner."

"I'm counting on it, because he said he'd be bringing the pizza."

"That reminds me. I have to stop for beer."

He had just said goodbye and was heading for the stairs when he heard his name called. It was not Margaret; it was Mike. "Coming down," Kevin replied. At the foot of the stair, he suggested that they sit on the steps of the front porch and bring each other up to date. As they walked out the door, Kevin showed Mike the ledger. "This is a record of sales stops Stanley made, starting in 1981 and then into 1983."

"How did you miss it before?" Mike asked as the two men sat down on the step.

"It dropped behind a cover that had been put over one of the hot water radiators in the tower room. I'm not sure if it has any bearing on the case, but who knows?"

"Well, then, listen to what I've discovered. It took a lot of searching, but I found that the case file had been mislabeled. It was filed under the name Stanley Bradshaw, and it contained the coroner's report I'd never seen. Nothing was ever said in the press releases, but according to the coroner, Stanley sustained a blow to the head that would have cracked his skull and rendered him unconscious. The coroner speculated that the blow preceded the stab wounds, and that those wounds were made by a thick blade, like that of a hunting knife. There was a lot of internal bleeding. That, added to the head injury, made everything work against Stanley's pulling through."

"Did you find a match for the unidentified Steven who was in the family photos?"

"No luck, and Officer Bud Matthews, the gay cop, even double-checked for me."

"Did you check on reports of gay bashing?"

"There were a couple of reports, but it was mostly verbal abuse and some shoving. Nothing even close to the brutality of Stan's murder."

"Any chance I could talk with Officer Matthews?"

"Sure, he's eager to help. In fact, he should still be at the station. Hop in my car and I'll drive."

* * * * *

At the station Chief Nicholas Harris invited Kevin, Mike and Officer Bud Matthews to use his office. "I think you should sit in on this, Nick," Mike stated. The Chief agreed, and the four men sat down behind a closed door.

Kevin did not hesitate to start. "I think we need to know where gay men hang out in this town. Since Stan was gay, there might be some older men who remember him . . . men with whom he'd been associating."

The Bud grinned. "A gay bar in Bedford? That'll never happen in this conservative town. Most of the guys party at a bar in Findley. What a difference thirty miles can make! The bar is on Main Street in the middle of town, and even now in Bedford, the gay community remains paranoid about the local cops."

Chapter Seven

Kevin's visit to the police station with Mike, the retired detective, proved productive. The current and open minded, Chief Harris met with Kevin, Mike and Bud, the openly gay police officer. They had talked of the town's conservative nature and the gay bar located in an adjacent, more liberal, community.

"Do many older guys show up at the bar?" Chief Harris asked. "Mr. Morgan would be about sixty-five now, right?"

"In answer to your first questions, there are more young guys than older ones. As to your second question, yes, Mr. Morgan would be in his middle sixties. With regard to the age of the men showing up at the bar, it helps to remember that it's not unusual for there to be a ten or even twenty year difference between the ages of partners."

"So then, the question might be, do men who are fifty, give or take a few years, sometimes show up?"

"Oh, yeah. There are guys in their fifties and sixties. Sometimes they're alone, and sometimes with a steady partner. But as I said, the majority of the guys are younger. Still, I'm sure there would be those who would remember Stanley Morgan."

"Could you take some pictures and some names to the bar and do some checking for us?" Kevin asked.

"They know I'm a cop, and I really doubt that I'd get straight answers." He chuckled at his own choice of adjective. "And, if you think the murderer might be gay, and if the Steve your looking for is still hanging around, my questions could scare them off. We surely don't want to do that."

"I'll go undercover." Kevin stated.

The three men laughed.

"I'm serious."

"You could pass," the gay officer said, winking at Kevin, who blushed. "There," the officer said. "That's what'll give you away. If you're not comfortable with men coming onto you, your cover will be blown. The only way it might work is if you went with another man who could run interference for you," Officer Matthews suggested. "No one will hit on you if you appear to be with a partner. Do you know a gay man who would go with you?"

"No, and I'm not sure where to start looking for one, but give me the address of the bar and I'll see what I can do."

"Wait," Chief Harris said. "You do understand that if you do this, you're on your own. If you get into trouble, there won't be any backup waiting to rush in to rescue you. If you'll tell us whatever you learn, and if I feel it's at all substantial, I'll consider reopening the case. Right now, however, the case is closed, and it'll stay that way, unless or until you can convince me otherwise."

"That's fair," Kevin responded.

Mike stayed on to tell the chief of the misfiling of the case and the unreported autopsy findings. Bud walked Kevin to the front desk, where he wrote out the bar's address and wished him luck. "Oh, one more thing," the officer added. "If I see you at the bar, I'm going to ignore you. Don't take it personally."

"Oh, darn," Kevin said with a limp wrist gesture. Both men laughed at the overused stereotype.

* * * * *

Kevin arrived home by five, bearing two six-packs of beer. While he cleaned up and changed out of his work clothes, Cathy looked through the Stan's ledger. "I've also been reading more of Margaret's diary. She turned into one really sensual woman." Cathy giggled before she continued. "Her language was so innocent, but she still made it pretty clear that she and John loved their intimate activities. They named their son after his Great-Uncle Stanley. Did you know her uncle was a contractor and built that house for himself, but gave it to Margaret as a wedding present?"

Kevin was about to respond when the door bell rang. He went to let Mike in.

Over hot pepperoni pizza and cold beer, the three summarized their days and their discoveries. Kevin praised the help of Bud, the homosexual cop. He also expressed appreciation of the current Chief Harris. Former Chief Bailey's name came up several times in a less-than-complimentary context. It was Mike who told of Kevin's idea about going to the gay bar in Findley, and Cathy teased about him finally coming out. She then offered to go with him.

"That wouldn't work, hon."

"I just feel a need to protect your virtue," she replied.

"I do have to find either a gay man or a good actor who will go with me as my pretend-lover."

Neither Mike nor Cathy could come up with a name. At 9:00, Mike left, and the pizza boxes and empty beer cans were deposited in the recycling bins on the back porch.

"I love you, Kevin," Cathy said as they curled up on the couch to watch the news. It was not long before they were cleaned up and in bed, where they snuggled with Buster curled up at their feet. All three slept soundly.

* * * * *

The morning had already begun to warm up as Kevin sat nursing a cup of coffee while waiting for Bill. He and his co-worker had a moving job, one for a couple moving from an apartment into a small house on the other side of town. It would be an easy job, and Kevin hoped to be home by mid-afternoon. Cathy sat at the table with him, casually leafing through the pictures that still covered most of the surface. "J," she said out of the blue. "We need to figure out if that initial J has any significance."

"And I've got to somehow get to the bar in Findley to see if anyone recognizes that Steven in the pictures. But trying to track down just a J seems impossible. It could be Jerry, Jim, Jason or two dozen other names beginning with that initial."

"Or even maybe Janet or Jane or a couple dozen female names. We don't know if Stan was a switch hitter or if Margaret was referring to one of her own friends. Those entries were very vague. I sure wish ghosts had phones."

Just then their phone rang. "I hate it when that happens," Kevin stated as he lifted the wall phone from its receiver. "Hello." There was a pause as he listened. "Oh. Hi, Bill. That's okay, take your time. Cathy and I are just sitting here talking about that mystery I'd mentioned to you briefly." After saying goodbye and hanging up the phone, he turned to his wife, who was pouring herself another cup of coffee. "Bill's going to be a few minutes late. He has to drop his kids off at school."

"What does his wife do?"

"I don't know. All I know is that he's no longer married."

"Oh. Well, I'm going to hop in the shower. Yell goodbye before you leave." Having kissed Kevin, she headed for the bathroom, carrying her coffee.

Kevin added dry food to Buster's metal food dish, the sound causing the cat to dash in from the living room. Kevin then switched on the small kitchen TV. The channel had somehow been turned to a local news station that was reporting that a brown bear had been spotted on the edge of town, a very rare sighting. The doorbell rang just as the story ended. Kevin chugged down the rest of his coffee, yelled goodbye to Cathy, and went to the door to greet the man who would help him with the moving.

Kevin's burly co-worker left his car parked at the curb. Together, they rode in Kevin's van. It was a short distance to the first floor apartment, and the loading went quickly. The couple had already transferred most of their clothing, personal items and smaller objects. The two men agreed to have lunch at a Chinese buffet, where Bill stacked his plate higher than did Kevin. Bill, who was in his mid-fifties, was a big man with a big appetite.

"I had a dream last night. A young cop told me I had a special assignment to somehow help you."

Kevin figured it was a message from Margaret. "What did the cop say to do?"

"He told me *you* would tell me what I had to do. So, tell me more about this mystery you and Cathy are working on."

"I'm not sure how much I mentioned before, but twenty-five years ago a man was murdered in Bedford. There were no good clues, but a detective named Mike was determined not to give up. The police chief back then stopped the investigation, how-ever, because the victim was a homosexual. The murder got written off as a hate crime, was misfiled under the wrong name, and then stashed away as a cold case."

"Hmmm. I'd have been in my twenties back then," Bill said, "and I think I remember that case. The victim was stabbed, wasn't he? And then he lived on for a few days in the hospital?"

"Yeah, he never regained consciousness. The autopsy report stated that he was struck in the head before being stabbed, but that report never was made public. In fact, the investigating detective was totally unaware of it."

"All because of the chief's prejudice. I remember hearing about that old SOB, and a lot of people were glad to see him go. I think that was sometime in 1985." Bill's anger was apparent. "But why your sudden interest in this old case, Kevin?"

"You probably won't believe this, Bill, but Cathy and I have seen the ghost of the man's mother. I know this'll sound crazy, but we honestly believe she's very lonely, and will not be free to join her son and her husband until Stanley's murderer is found."

Bill gazed at Kevin as though trying to see inside the younger man's head. "I believe you, and I want to help, but I'm not sure how I can."

"I almost hate to ask this, but here goes. Do you think you might be able to pretend you're gay, and go with me to a gay bar in Findley? We think Stanley used to go there, and I'd like to ask around to see what I could discover. I have pictures of a man named Steven who we think was Stan's lover for a while. We don't think he's the murderer, but he might have some information that could help. We also have the initial J, but we don't know if it even fits into the puzzle."

"Let me get this straight. You want me to act like a homosexual and go as your partner to this gay bar, right?" Bill's laugh was robust.

"Yeah. I hate to ask you to pretend to be gay."

"Pretend? I thought you knew."

"Knew what?"

"I *am* gay."

"But you have kids."

"Like a lot of guys, I was married for a while before I finally accepted my orientation. My ex-wife and I remain friends, though, and my teenagers are finally old enough to understand."

"Wow, this is perfect. If I'm with you, I won't need to worry that some guy will hit on me."

"And I can guarantee that if you went into that bar alone, guys would definitely be hitting on you." Bill chuckled at Kevin's obvious discomfort.

"I guess that would be better than being attacked by a bear. Did you see on the news that one had been spotted on the edge of town?"

"Hey, Kevin, you're sitting with one."

"What?"

"There are furry brown bears that hang around the edge of town, and there are hairy gay bears that hang around the bar in Findley. In the gay community, big guys like me are called bears."

"Somehow Margaret told me that on the news. Now, do I need to worry about making anyone jealous by doing this?"

"Naw. I'll clear it with my partner. Not to worry, he'll understand."

* * * * *

Kevin excitedly told Cathy that he had found a pretend-partner to go with him to the bar.

"Wow, I'm not surprised that Bill was eager to help, but I never figured him for gay. You said he was married and has kids."

"It took him a while to accept his orientation. You know, it must be tough being gay and having to grow up in a society that expects everyone to be straight."

"Well, at least he knew what to do with a woman when he was married, unlike the cop in my dream."

"Oh, that was probably Margaret's message about Detective Mike's investigation being blocked by Chief Bailey. In the dream Bill had, the cop told him to help us out."

"Margaret's ghost is very cryptic, but the woman was clearly very tolerant and understanding. I would like to have had her as a friend."

"Hard telling what kind of mischief you and Margaret would have gotten into."

"Speaking of mischief, do remember that you need to inform Mike of your and Bill's agenda, so he can pass that on to Chief Harris."

"I'll call him soon so there's still time for him to catch the chief at the station."

"I know Mike will appreciate your keeping him posted. I'm sure Margaret and John appreciated how frustrated he was when he was pulled off the case and it was closed. I think he needs the closure almost as much as Margaret and John do."

"I heard that Chief Bailey is still alive and living in an institution. If we solve this, I'm going to tell that prejudiced SOB. I think he needs to know that he didn't stop the search fpr justice."

"So, you're really going to the bar tonight? Are you ready for this?"

"I don't want to start asking questions too quickly. I think that would seem strange. Bill's going to be perfect for this, because he knows the bar. He says that if he's with me, I'll be better able to get information from the guys who might not otherwise want to share with a stranger."

"While you worked this morning, I re-read some of the diary entries during the months following the murder. Somehow I missed a couple of angry references to 'C B'. I was confused, because years earlier Margaret had mentioned a cousin named Christopher Bennington. Now, though, I think her venom must have been directed at Chief Bailey. Often, in the context of her anger, she wrote of having to scream out loud and then of crying herself to sleep."

"'Ain't it a shame. My tears fell like rain.'"

Changing the subject, Cathy asked, "Have you thought about what you'll wear tonight?"

"No, I haven't. Any suggestions?"

"What do I know? I'd guess, however, that a gay man with your build would want to show off his body. Wear a tight T-shirt and those old short shorts that have been in the bottom drawer for years."

"If I can still get into them."

"When's Bill coming to pick you up?"

"Around 8:30. It will take us about forty-five minutes to get there. He says things start to hop between 9:00 and 9:30."

"You'll probably get home late."

"Yeah, unless you tell Bill he has to have me home by midnight."

"Just be sure you come home."

"I'll always come home." Having smiled and winked, Kevin picked up the phone and called Mike. The retired detective sounded excited by the news that the plan was beginning to unfold. He promised Kevin that he would also notify Chief Harris. After he hung up, Cathy suggested a nap. The two snuggled under a light cover. They hadn't set the alarm, but both woke spontaneously after sleeping soundly for about ninety minutes. They were still cuddling when they woke, and only separated when Buster let them know that he wanted some loving also.

Dinner consisted of pizza left over from the night Mike brought it with him. Cathy added a salad to the menu and topped things off with easy-bake sugar cookies. After dinner, Kevin showered and she finished cleaning up the kitchen. Having poured two cups of coffee, she went quietly into the bathroom, although without meaning to surprise him. He was in fact surprised, however, for she walked in as he was checking himself out in the mirror..

"Looks like you're getting ready for a hot date," she joked.

"No, I wanted fo see how these shorts looked."

* * * * *

Shortly after he finished dressing, the doorbell sounded. "That's my date," Kevin announced.

Cathy stood at her husband's side when he opened the door. Bill somehow looked bigger than when he wore his work clothes. He was also wearing shorts, but had on a muscle shirt. The low neck revealed a dark patch of chest hair.

"Good evening, Mrs. Riley," he said.

"Good evening, Bill. Now, you be sure you don't keep my Kevin out too late tonight."

"Don't worry, Mrs. Riley. I'll have your boy home early."

Kevin hugged Cathy and kissed her. She followed them out onto the front porch, where she stood watching them drive away. She waved, knowing neither would see her. "Just you and I tonight, big guy," she said to Buster who was sitting at her feet.

* * * * *

Most of the drive was in silence, but Kevin expressed a bit of anxiety as they drove into Findley.

"You're not homophobic, are you?" Bill asked.

"No, Bill. No problem there."

Bill placed his right hand on Kevin's knee. "For this to be believable, I will have to touch you once in a while. Will that be okay?"

"I can handle it," Kevin replied as he placed his left hand on Bill's knee. As they pulled into the bar's parking lot, Kevin felt sure that they would pull off their act. His confidence wavered, however, as they walked into the bar where men were dancing together. Bill grabbed his hand, and Kevin's confidence returned.

Chapter Eight

Bill continued to hold Kevin's hand as they walked into the gay bar in the town of Findley.

"We'll sit at the bar," Bill said loud enough be to heard over the music "Let me order for you." As they walked in that direction, Bill nodded hellos to a few men he knew. They all seemed to be checking out his hot date. Kevin hoped he was not blushing.

At the bar, Bill greeted the bartender by name. "Evening, Bruce."

"What'll it be for the two of you, Bill?"

"A couple of draft beers."

The bartender placed a bowl of unshelled peanuts in front of them. Kevin had noticed that there were peanut shells scattered around, and he followed Bill's lead when he cracked open a peanut and dropped the shell on the floor. When the bartender returned with the beers, Bill had a question. "How long have you been working here, Bruce?"

"I started tending bar when I was twenty-one, and I'm thinking of retiring next year. Of course, when I started, we were in a smaller building, tucked away on a side street. I've been at this for thirty-odd years. That's a lot of standing, and these old legs are about to give out."

"Another question, then. Kevin and I have become interested in the murder of a gay man in Bedford. I guess it was about twenty-five years ago. I think he might have come to this bar."

Bill had certainly jumped right into the questioning, and Kevin held his breath, trusting that the older man knew what he was doing. The bartender could be a valuable source of information.

"Oh, yeah, I remember that. In fact, when he died we held a memorial service here for him. Even his mother and dad came. It was all so emotional, the tears flowed like rain. I'll tell you something, but you'll think I'm crazy."

"Probably not," Kevin said.

"Be right back. Gotta see what Terry wants." After mixing Terry a whisky sour, Bruce came back and leaned over the bar. "We held that service on the seventh of August. We had one minute of silence at eleven o'clock. Now, this will sound bizarre, but every seventh of August since then, at exactly eleven o'clock, that neon beer sign over the cash register mysteriously goes off for a full minute and then flickers back on again. I swear there is some spirit or something that wants us to never forget." A tear rolled down the bartender's cheek. He wiped it away with a paper napkin and continued. "You see, his parents believed his murderer would never be found because no one cared. It was just one less fag in the conservative town of Bedford."

"We don't think you're crazy, Bruce," Kevin said as he laid his hand on that of the bartender.

"Some of us did care, and a lot of us still care," the bartender said.

"We want to find the SOB who killed him," Bill said. "There has to be some justice."

"And closure for his family," Kevin added.

Bruce was called away again by a man ordering two glasses of red wine, and then he refilled the bowl of peanuts in front of two men who were obviously feeling an attraction for each other. When he returned, he again leaned over the bar and said in a soft voice, "I don't want you to think that this is some kind of cult, but on every anniversary of that memorial meeting, men show up here who might only come on that one special night. Originally we had a couple of dozen who would gather in that corner to remember." He nodded in the direction of a corner with two large round tables and ten empty chairs. "That number has dwindled over the years. For the past two, only six of the old timers showed up."

"Do you remember the name of the man who was murdered?" Kevin asked.

"Yeah. It was Stan," the bartender replied.

"Morgan," Kevin said before the bartender could finish. "It was Stan Morgan and his mother was Margaret."

"And his father was John," the bartender was quick to insert before being drawn off again by a thirsty customer. He only returned to ask if more beer or peanuts were needed then returned to the bar to wash beer mugs.

Kevin saw the gay police officer, Bud, but they avoided each other's eyes. Kevin noted that most of the men there were young. Many had not even been born yet, or else were still in preschool, when the crime occurred. "I'm not sure what more we'll learn tonight," he said to Bill.

"How about one dance before we head for home, just for appearances?"

Kevin consented, and Bill took him by the hand and led him to the dance floor. It was a slow dance, and Bill wrapped his big arms around his date. Kevin allowed the bear to lead. They then walked by the bar and said goodnight to Bruce. On the way out, Bill nodded to a couple of men he recognized. Outside the bar, Bill let go of Kevin's hand. "Next week we'll come on Thursday night. That seems to be the busiest night, and more men my age will show up. We'll see if any of them can identify the man in the pictures. I would have asked Bruce, but he got busy. We'll check with him next time."

They talked only about work schedules on the way home. Tomorrow would be a light day, and Kevin would work alone. He hoped he would have time to check on the addresses in Stanley's business-call ledger. He would also find time to talk with Mike. Right now, however, he wanted to get home to Cathy.

It was 12:45 when Kevin walked into his home. Cathy, who had been dozing on the couch, jumped up to greet him. After a long kiss, she asked, "Did you learn anything at the bar . . . About Stanley, I mean."

"We only talked to the bartender. Most of the other men there were way too young to remember anything from the time Stan would have been there. But Bruce, the bartender, had vivid memories of not only Stan, but of his mother and father. Shortly after Stanley's death, a memorial was held in the bar, and Margaret and John attended. Now there's an annual gathering on the August date."

"Tell me more about that annual gathering."

"It's just that some of the old timers gather, and for some, that is the only night they come to the bar. The highlight of the evening is when the neon beer sign over the bar goes dark for a full minute at eleven o'clock. The bartender said that the number showing up has steadily declined over the years, but six or eight men still show up."

"I worry about reliable sources of information dwindling away each year, too. And, speaking of dwindling, tomorrow I've got to buy some groceries. We've been preoccupied with this case, and our food supply is declining steadily."

"I could meet for lunch if you'd like, but then I'm want to check out some of the addresses in Stan's ledger."

"Let's plan on having lunch here. Then I think it might make more sense to see what you can find by comparing the ledger with the phonebook first. The county yellow pages cover Cruxton, Bedford and Findley, and that should pretty much cover things."

Kevin agreed that made better sense, rather than running all over the county without knowing what businesses were still in business and in the same location.

As they lay in bed, Kevin told of the plans to return to the bar with Bill on Thursday, the busiest night of the week. Then he hoped he might try to learn about Steven and possibly someone with a name beginning with J. They fell asleep quickly after saying goodnight to Buster.

* * * * *

The morning was uneventful for each of them. His job was simply to help move supplies and furniture from a first floor office to another on the second floor. His padding, his dolly and his muscles were required, but not his brain. He found himself briefly thinking about the novel he had hoped to write some day. What had seemed to be a high priority had recently been shoved to a back burner. *Once this is all over, I'll have time to again start thinking about writing.*

Having arrived home before noon, he helped Cathy prepare lunch. She made the cheese sandwiches while he stirred the tomato soup to keep it from sticking to the bottom of the pan. She was chief chef and he was her assistant, except when it came to making his infamous baked beans.

Right after lunch he called Mike. After telling him about the annual gathering, the retired detective asked a very logical question, which neither Bill nor Kevin had thought of. "Did you get a list of the men who have been coming to that yearly event?"

"Darn it, Mike, I didn't. I didn't get a chance to have him look at pictures, either, but Bill and I are going back next week. Thursday is supposed to be a good night for older men to show up. I also need to see if anyone can come up with someone who has a first or last name starting with J, or who simply goes by that initial."

Mike asked to be kept informed and promised to call Chief Harris to fill him in on the scanty information. When he hung up, Cathy had already brought the phone book to the table, along with the ledger, a pen and a pad of paper. "You crosscheck, and I'll write down the businesses that are still open," Cathy suggested.

"Sounds good to me." He looked at the first page and then the second. "We can do this first, but I'll still need to do some driving around, because some of these entries are addresses only, without a business name."

"Are we wasting our time?" Cathy wondered out loud. "I'm not sure checking out the stops he made while peddling sweepers is going to tell us anything."

"What else can we do? All we have to work on right now is the information from the gay bar and what's in this ledger. I think we've learned all we can from the family pictures and Margaret's diary. After all, Margaret did heat up that iron, and it was the concept of something hot that got me checking behind the radiator covers. She must have felt that this ledger is somehow important. Mike's been able to add the missing autopsy report, so we've learned that Stan was probably knocked unconscious with a blow to his head before he was stabbed with a hunting knife."

"Oh! Quick, look through those pages," Cathy suggested. "Is there a hunting store listed?"

"Yeah, it seems that in May of 1982, he stopped at the Wilderness Hunting Supply Store in Findley, and then again in August of the same year."

"It's still in business," Cathy reported after finding its listing in the phonebook.

"And a Deer Run Hunting Shop. That was in December of 1982. Is it still on Mulberry Street in Bedford?"

"Nope, not in the phone book, but there is a Fireside Hunting and Camping Outlet in Bedford. It's on Hamilton Road." Carrying the phonebook with her, she walked to the kitchen wall phone and punched in the outlet's number. When the call was answered, Cathy replied, "I'm with a company putting together a history of businesses in Bedford. Do you recall the Deer Run Shop?" She shook her head and Kevin knew the answer to her question was "No."

"Can you tell me when your store opened?" There was a pause. "Well, you're fairly new. Thanks for your time." She hung up and returned to the table. "1995."

"Back to the drawing board."

"Let's think about this. What else was found in the autopsy that could be a lead?"

"I'll call Mike to see if there was anything he forgot to tell me." From the wall phone, Kevin entered Mike's number, but got his answering machine. "Hi, Mike. I hate to keep bothering you, but Cathy and I wonder if there was anything else in that autopsy report that might provide a clue – anything you might have forgotten to mention. We're grasping at straws right now, so anything is good, Mike. Anything you can add might form a piece to this puzzle. Give me a call when you get a chance."

They returned to the cross-referencing of ledger with phone book, finding a cheese shop, a gospel book store, an attorney's office and a beauty parlor still open in Cruxton. A Findley hardware store, a meat market, an office supply store, a barber shop, and a men's clothing store were apparently still in business. Also listed was the gay bar, but at its original location. A garden supply store, feed mill and the coffee shop where Kevin first met Mike were on Stanley's route list and still listed in the Bedford section of the yellow pages. Over half of the businesses in Stan's ledger had apparently closed.

Having listed all the existing businesses, Cathy got up and turned on the burner under the tea kettle. "Black or green?"

"What?"

"Tea. Do you want black or green tea?"

"I'll have green."

"Ouch!" Cathy had reached back without looking, and steam from the kettle had singed her hand.

"You okay?"

"More surprised than burned. I didn't expect the steam this soon."

"Steam." Kevin looked through the ledger pages. "When you take your clothes to the cleaners, what to you see?" He answered his own question. "Steam. They clean with steam and they press with steam. Starlight Cleaners was in business in Bedford
back in '81. According to his ledger, Stanley visited it only once,. Who knows when it closed? Steam might be a clue, and maybe this business has some real significance."

"Or maybe I was just your wishful thinking. Let's try not to get obsessed and start making false assumptions."

Just then the phone rang. It was Mike returning Kevin's call. "Hang on, Mike. I want to grab another phone. With that one, Cathy and I can both hear you on speaker phone." Cathy carefully turned off the burner under the tea kettle. They went into the living room, where Kevin lifted the phone and hit a button. "Okay, Mike. We can both hear you now."

"First: this news. I found out that former Chief Bailey is indeed still alive, but he is, as we suspected, in the mental hospital there in Cruxton. Then, you were wondering about the autopsy report. I told you that the coroner speculated that the stab wounds suggested a hunting knife as opposed to the thinner blade of a kitchen knife. I told you how he found evidence of a blow to the head with a blunt instrument and gave you his generic description of the weapon. Well, I also found another notation. I might not have told you that the bruise on Stanley's forehead was described as being the shape of a garden trowel."

"That last bit is news to us. Stanley's ledger shows he had visited a farmer's supply store, a garden shop, and a hardware store. A couple are still in business, but I'm not sure what I can learn from any of his listings. Twenty-five years – a lot of staff turnover's bound to have happened."

After saying goodbye to Mike, Cathy and Kevin continued sitting on the couch. "I'm feeling a bit discouraged."

"Me too," Cathy replied. "Leads keep popping up, but a lot of them fizzle out."

"And so much has changed in a quarter of a century. Damn, for all we know, the killer is dead or living in Mexico. We need something exciting to happen."

Just then the phone rang. It was still on speaker phone when Cathy answered. "Hey, girl, this is Julie. I've got to tell you about the hot date I had last night."

Cathy put her finger to her lips, advising Kevin to be quiet and just listen. "Tell me about it."

"Well, it was a blind date: the brother of a gal at work. Since she's a pretty good-looking woman, I figured that her brother couldn't be too bad. Damn, Cathy, that guy was hot, hot, hot! When I opened my door and looked up into those blue eyes, my heart skipped a couple beats."

"Wow," Cathy remarked, winking at Kevin. "But call me later. No time to talk."

"I'll call you tomorrow," Julie said.

After saying goodbye, Cathy turned to Kevin. That's not the kind of exciting news I was wanting to hear."

The two finished up checking the ledger against the county yellow pages, and Kevin laid out his tentative plans for visiting some of the location in the morning. They were both feeling tired and after dinner, relaxed for a while and then hit the sack early. Neither, however, got a good night's sleep.

The restlessness both experienced in the morning was the result of frequently being awaked by disturbing dreams, only to fall asleep again and have the dream repeat itself.

"Damn," Kevin said even before the alarm went off. "That was a terrible night. I kept dreaming of being locked up with no escape. The guards were dressed in white uniforms, and no matter how much I pleaded with them, they wouldn't let me go."

"Where did you say Chief Bailey is now?"

"Oh, my God. He's in a mental hospital. Those weren't guards in white uniforms – those were attendants. I need to see that man. I need to talk with the SOB."

"The dream I kept having was of me trying to sew up a rip in something I couldn't identify, but every time I'd sew in a stitch, it would come out again. I think we both experienced a sense of frustration, but only a taste of what Stanley's parents must have felt."

"And, Cathy, didn't you read me an entry from the diary in which Margaret had cryptically said something about something coming unstitched?"

"Wow, yes. That sure fits with my dream, but the meaning's still a mystery."

"Well, one thing I know for sure. I've got to go talk with that Bailey guy in the psych hospital."

* * * * *

After breakfast Kevin called Mike. "I'm going to go see the former chief, and I'm wondering if you have any more information I should have before I talk with him."

"From what I've heard," Mike replied, "you'll not speak with him, only to him. I guess he's become pretty incoherent."

"Alzheimer's, or something like that?"

"No, the story is he had a mental breakdown sometime in the fall of '83, but was able to keep it under some control for a couple years. Then around '85 or '86 he just went totally berserk, ranting and raving. But let me call you back. I need to check something with Chief Harris first."

Mike did not even hint at what he need to talk to the chief about, and Kevin did not have a chance to ask.

"Geeze, Cathy. It sounds like old Chief Bailey is really bonkers," Kevin said. "Plus I'm a little confused by how Mike ended our conversation. He said he's got to check with Chief Harris about something, but I have no idea what. The mysteries continue."

Chapter Nine

Kevin was expecting a return call from Mike, the detective, but took advantage of the break to call work and talk with the dispatcher to learn if he had any pickup orders. After hanging up, he filled Cathy in on his schedule. "I'll need to spend tomorrow moving a family's furniture into a storage unit. The guy's been transferred, and they still don't have a place to live, but he's moving his family into a furnished apartment."

"Will that be an all day job?"

"Most of it, probably, so if I can't get to the psych hospital to talk with old Chief Bailey tomorrow, I'll do it the next day."

Just then the phone rang. Cathy, who was closest to it, answered. "Oh, hi, Mike. Hang on, and I'll put you on speaker phone so you and Kev can talk."

"Hi, Mike," Kevin said. "What's up?"

"You can't go to see Chief Bailey. His family has requested no visitors and the doctors have agreed that visitors would only upset him. Chief Harris has pulled some strings, though. He'll be able to talk with him, but he'll have to go alone. Sorry, Kevin."

"Not your fault, Mike. I guess we'll just have to wait to hear what Harris finds out."

"That will probably be sometime late this afternoon. It was good of him to make time in his busy schedule. He's beginning to understand how important this is, not just to us, but for the reputation of the department."

They thanked Mike for his information and goodbyes were exchanged.

"While we're waiting to hear," Cathy said after hanging up, "let's look one more time at the undated pictures we couldn't get into sequence. Then we can put everything into envelopes and mark each with the year."

There were only about a dozen pictures that could not be identified, at least approximately, by year. Kevin spread them out, face up, and immediately picked one up. "This scene I recognize. Well, the neon beer sign and Bruce the bartender at a much younger age. This must have been in the old bar, but they took that neon sign to the new location. It's the one that goes off every year in memory of Stan's death. This bowl here on the bar is no doubt filled with unshelled peanuts and this box with condoms."

"This is off the wall, Kevin, and I'm sure I'm adding two and two and coming up with seven. Look at the picture and think of how a lot of people would describe the old chief and the confinement he's in."

At a loss, Kevin just shook his head.

"The old guy's nuts and is locked up in a rubber room."

Kevin's snicker was echoed by another, a softer one from somewhere in the room. "Lady, you are wacko. But the photo does verify that Stan was a patron, the bartender was indeed around when Stan was, the neon sign dates back into the 80's, and they were advocating safe sex even back then."

The picture from the old bar was estimated to belong somewhere in the '81 pile, but Kevin kept it out to show Bruce. An older one showing Stanley as a young boy in kickers was put in the pile with others in which he was wearing similar attire. By three o'clock, everything was sorted and filed away in brown envelopes.

"I'm ready for a nap," Kevin announced.

"Me, too. Should I take the phone off the hook?"

"No, if Chief Harris calls, I want to get it."

The two went into the bedroom with Buster close behind. When serious about their naps they would strip completely, and today they were serious. They snuggled, kissed, wished each other pleasant dreams, and fell asleep.

It was almost six o'clock when the phone woke them. Kevin rolled over and picked up the one on the bed stand. "Hello." He was silent for a minute, listening as the Chief wondered about a meeting. "Sure, Chief, we can meet here. Cathy and I still need to eat, so would eight o'clock work for you?"

After exchanging goodbyes, Kevin hung up the phone and rolled back over to hold the warm body of his wife. "He wants to come by to talk with us. He says he took a tape recorder in with him, and what is recorded is something he can't describe. He says we have to hear it for ourselves."

Together they threw together a quick dinner of bacon and eggs, topped off with large bowls of moose tracks ice cream. Their bodies and their kitchen were cleaned up when the door bell rang a few minutes before eight. "Hi Chief! Any problem finding our house?"

"My GPS brought me right to it. I'm glad you could see me tonight. I couldn't have slept, had I not had the chance to talk with you."

"Come on in," Cathy invited. "I have fresh coffee, if you're in the mood."

"I'm always in the mood for good coffee, and yours has to be an improvement over what I get at the station. Let's just sit here at the kitchen table."

"Cream and sugar, Chief?"

"Just cream, and my name is Nick, Mrs. Riley."

"Cream it is, and just call me Cathy, then."

Kevin motioned toward the table. "And I'm eager to find out what you learned."

The chief waited until Cathy sat down, at which point he placed his tape recorder in the middle of the table and sat down also. "Now, picture this. Chief Bailey is seventy-nine, skinny as a rail, and dressed in a one-piece, pocketless, beltless outfit. I walk in to his room through a locked door which is closed behind me. A burly attendant is stationed just outside the room. Lester, ah, Chief Bailey, is pacing and does not seem to be aware that I've come into the room. I'll start the recording. I hope it's not too upsetting, Cathy."

"I'm ready," she replied.

Chief Harris pressed the start button, and the first voice was his. "Lester, it's me, Nicholas. Nicholas Harris."

A weaker voice rasped, "Tell her to stop. She never stops. All night, all day, can't sleep. Make her stop screaming. She won't stop. Tell her, tell her to stop."

"Who's screaming? Tell me who it is."

"Make her stop. Make her stop screaming."

"Who is it that's screaming? Tell me, and maybe I can make her stop."

Lester's voice increased in volume. "You're not the one. You can't stop her. Stop, please stop. She won't let me sleep – her endless screaming."

"What is she screaming?"

"Just screaming. Listen, you'll hear her screaming. She's screaming! Make her stop. Please make her stop. All day all night, never stopping. Endless screaming. Stop her."

"How can I get her to stop?"

"You're not the one. You can't make her stop. Why does she keep screaming?"

Chief Harris stopped the recording. "It goes on like this for another ten minutes – just the same pathetic plea to make her stop screaming. Several times he told me I'm not the one, but I didn't know what he meant by that."

"He does sound pretty mental – hearing voices," Cathy said.

"Not voices. Just screaming," the chief stated. "But I heard her too. It was just hysterical screaming, full of pain and anger. No words, but definitely a woman's voice. I didn't realize that the recorder wasn't recording the screams, until I listened to it on my way home from the institution."

"Do you think it was another patient?" Kevin asked, not really believing that it was.

"That's what I thought at first, so when I came out of the room I asked the attendant who was doing all that screaming, but all I got was this blank look. He asked me what screaming I was talking about, and I told him it was some woman. He then said that was impossible, as the male and female wards are separate, with the women's being one floor up."

"So what are you thinking now?"

"I'd guess it was Margaret Morgan."

The chief's mention of Margaret surprised Cathy and Kevin. "How did you think of her?"

"Mike has told me all about her ghost, and all about how involved you are in trying to solve this cold case. I was skeptical until I heard her anger-and-pain-filled screams."

"You said Bailey kept saying you're not the one . . . you're not the man. I don't want to come across as crazy as he is, but I have a feeling that I'm the one who can get her to stop screaming. I just need to figure out how." He nervously tapped his fingers on the table.

Cathy reached across and squeezed Kevin's. hand. "Relax," she said, "I'm on your team." .

Chief Harris reached across and placed his hand on top of theirs. "I am too. Let me know of any way I or my department can help. You know Bud wants to stay involved."

"Mike's on the team also," Cathy said.

"And so is a hairy gay man named Bill."

"What a team! A small town police chief, a retired detective, a gay bear, an aspiring author and a music teacher." Cathy giggled and so did Margaret. All three heard her, and each looked in a different direction, for she was nowhere, but at the same time everywhere.

"You're the man," Cathy said to her husband.

"You're the man," Chief Harris echoed.

Cathy and Kevin slept soundly, with their only dreams being whimsical. Kevin had a dream about selling his novel at a church bazaar and Cathy had a dream about taking in a stray cat. Each was ready to start the day when the alarm went off promptly at six. Over breakfast Cathy smiled and said, "I think Margaret is telling you your novel had better not be naughty."

Kevin spent the morning loading furniture with Bill's help. The only mention made of the time together in the gay bar was when Kevin mentioned the old photo of the old bar, but a younger Bruce. Bill asked if they had a date for Thursday night, and Kevin confirmed the plan and said he'd take the picture to show the bartender.

They then unloaded what they'd just loaded in a warehouse, where the items would stay until the family found a new home. Kevin was home a little after one, and Cathy met him at the door. "I have something exciting to tell you. Chief Harris called and said he could get you in to see the former chief. The question of why the case file was mislabeled and why the autopsy report was kept secret bugs him. He's hoping you can learn something of his predecessor's motivation."

"Did he say when?"

"He'll go with you this afternoon, if you're not worn out, or tomorrow afternoon, if that's better for you."

"I'm going to call him. I want to do it today. I think this is way more important than hitting businesses and checking out addresses written in the ledger. That can wait."

By the time Kevin cleaned up and changed out of his work clothes, Cathy had lunch waiting. After eating and relaxing with a cup of coffee, Kevin looked through the photographs from 1983. He selected one of Margaret that was dated just a week before Stanley was attacked. Holding it up, he announced, "I'm taking this one to show both the new chief and the old one." He then found one with Stan and the unidentified Steven. "I'll take this one, too."

* * * * *

Chief Harris arrived at the time agreed upon. They pulled into the institution's parking lot by three o'clock. "Remember, Kevin, this man's incoherent, and he's been so for over twenty years. Don't expect too much."

"This is something I have to do."

They checked in at a nursing station, and the husky attendant led the two men down a long, dim corridor, past a number of closed doors, each of which featured a little window. Stopping at the one behind which the former chief had spent the past two decades, the attendant hesitated. "For some reason Lester has been unusually agitated today. Remember, I'll be right outside the door if you need me."

On entering, Kevin was shocked at the sight of a frail-looking, gray-haired man who was looking at the floor and pacing from one side of the room to the other. "Make her stop screaming. She never stops – all day, all night. I can't sleep. Make her stop screaming, screaming, screaming!"

"Lester, it's me, Nick. Do you remember me?"

"Make her stop. Please make her stop screaming. She won't stop."

"I brought someone to meet you, Lester. His name's Kevin."

"Why won't she stop? Day and night, screaming, screaming." For the first time, he looked up and saw Kevin. The old man stumbled as he turned and headed toward Kevin. "You've come. You can make her stop. *Please* make her stop screaming. Please make her stop."

"How can I make her stop?" Kevin asked.

"You are the one. You can make her stop." Moving directly in front of Kevin, he took his hand.

The attendant, who had been watching through the small window, apparently was concerned, for he opened the door and stepped in. Chief Harris brought a finger to his lips and then motioned for him to leave.

"Do you hear her screaming? Make her stop. Please make her stop."

"I hear her. She sounds as if she's hurting and angry. Why is she so angry?"

"Evil." the old chief replied. "So much evil. The evil makes her angry."

The background sound of screaming grew louder. "What evil, Chief Bailey? What is the evil?"

"Make her stop. Too much evil." Letting go of Kevin's hand, he clasped his hands over his ears. "Oh, please. Make her stop."

"Is this who's screaming?" Kevin asked, holding out the picture of young Margaret.

Lester looked, and then quickly averted his eyes. "She won't stop. She's still screaming, but it's all evil. So much evil!"

Kevin then held out the photo of Stanley and the unidentified Steven. Before he could ask his question, Chief Bailey took one quick glance at it. He ran to a corner where he sank to the floor with hands clasped over his ears. "Evil, evil, evil. So much evil!"

Chief Harris touched Kevin's shoulder. "I think this is all we're going to get from him now. Let's get out of here."

Kevin walked to the crumpled man who was rocking and wailing in a corner. He knelt in front of him. "I want to make her stop – to end her pain. I will do all I can."

Lester looked up and made eye contact. In a soft voice, he said, "You must end the evil."

A moment more of eye contact and the man curled up again.

"I'll be back," Kevin said, touching the bony knee of the former Bedford police chief. There was no reply or acknowledgement.

Outside the door the attendant expressed his amazement. "I have never seen Lester show that kind of awareness." Looking at Kevin, he added, "He really seemed to connect with you. I couldn't believe it. How does he know you?"

"He doesn't. I've never seen him before in my life."

The attendant looked puzzled, and even more so when Chief Harris added, "He's the man."

On the way back the Chief offered to play the tape he had made in Lester's room, but Kevin suggested they wait and play it so Cathy could hear it, too. He called her on his cell phone.

"Chief Harris and I are on our way home with a recording I want you to hear. If you haven't eaten dinner and don't have anything prepared, we'll pick up fried chicken with all the trimmings."

Cathy accepted the offer, set the table for three and started the coffee. Then she waited. When Kevin walked in, she greeted him with a kiss and said hello to Nick.

Three hungry people made quick work of emptying the bucket of fried chicken and the mounds of mashed potatoes and coleslaw. The men refused Cathy's offer to put some easy-bake chocolate chip cookies in the oven, settling for just another cup of coffee.

Dishes were stacked in the sink, the three were seated and the recorder was placed in the middle of the table. As the tape began, Chief Harris stated, "We heard the woman's screams the whole time, but like last time they probably did not record."

A minute into the tape Cathy mused, "I wonder why it's so different this time."

The two men were puzzled. "In what way is it different?" Kevin asked.

"The screaming. This time it recorded."

"You hear it?" the chief asked.

"Sure. Don't you?"

Both men said, "No" at the same time.

"Spooky," Kevin said.

As the tape played, Cathy confided that she could hear the change in Lester's voice when he seemed to recognize Kevin. She also picked up on the introduction of the word evil when shown the picture of Stanley and Steven. "We need to learn more about this Steven," she commented.

"And there is still the mysterious J." Kevin added.

"But we do know who's screaming at Lester, and we can guess it's because he stopped the murder investigation of her son." The tape ended and the chief stroked his chin. "I wonder what will make her stop hurting?"

"Finding the killer," Kevin replied, and then repeated in a softer voice, "Finding the killer."

In silence the three team members finished their coffee.

Chapter Ten

Given that the next day was Sunday, the Rileys slept in. Kevin was the first to wake. Quietly, he slipped out of bed, headed for the coffee pot, turned on the kitchen TV and sat at the table.

Following a few local news reports, a photo of a uniformed police officer appeared on the screen. Kevin immediately recognized the person, despite the image of a much younger man. "The former Chief of the Bedford Police Department, Lester Bailey, was released last night from the hospital he entered in 1985. The family's attorney issued a written statement indicating only that Chief Bailey has been suffering a chronic illness and was released into the care of his daughter."

The short news report had no sooner ended when the phone rang. Kevin grabbed it after the first ring, hoping it did not wake Cathy. "Hello," he answered softly.

"Kevin, this is Nick, Chief Harris. I just heard on the news that . . . "

"I just heard it too. Bailey was released from the institution."

"I have a feeling he was not released. I think his daughter, for some reason, went and got him out against medical advice."

"Why would she do that?"

"I don't know, but I'll see what I can find out, and call you later today."

Kevin was hanging up the phone when he was surprised to hear Cathy's voice. He turned, to see his petite wife standing by the refrigerator. "Who was that calling so early on a Sunday morning?"

"That was Nick. It was just on TV that Bailey is out of the psych hospital. He and I both saw it."

"What? How did that happen?"

"All we know is that his daughter apparently went and got him. Nick's going to see what else he can find out and call back."

"Amazing."

"*You* are amazing, young lady. I never tire of seeing your beautiful body in the morning."

"Shut up and pour me some coffee. I'll check the freezer for those frozen waffles and get out some of the blueberries."

"Kevin was pouring Cathy's cup of coffee when the phone range. He answered the one sitting on the nightstand. It was Chief Harris.

"Wait, Chief, I want to put you on speaker phone so Cathy can hear also."

Together they moved quickly to the living room where they could switch on the speaker. "Hello, Nick," Cathy said.

"Hi, Cathy. I wanted to bring you two up to date. I know that facility's superintendent, Dr. Graham, pretty well from community meetings, so I called him at home. Now, he said he couldn't tell me everything, but then I think he did. Lester's daughter had been coming to visit her father about every two weeks, and she happened to come on the night we visited. The attendant was the one who told her of my first visit and then about the two of us coming. He also told her of how her father seemed to recognize you, how you had shown him pictures, and how Lester had ended up in the corner ranting about the evil."

"And because of that she took him home?"

"Dr. Graham said she was concerned that we had upset him, angry that the hospital had ignored her ban on visitors, and was afraid we would come back to harass her father. He said she even threatened to call her attorney if the institution did not comply. He said he had no choice but to release him, since he was no immediate threat to himself or to others."

"Wow! I wonder if his daughter took screaming Margaret Ann home also."

"Well," the Chief concluded, "we sure stirred something up."

After the three said goodbye, Cathy stood. "Let's go work on those waffles." Buster meowed because he was hungry.

After feeding Buster and eating waffles stacked with blueberries, Kevin helped clean up the few breakfast dishes, along with the few left over from last night's fried chicken dinner with Chief Nicholas Harris. Having helped make the bed, he then checked to see if Cathy would need the car.

"No," she answered. "I have laundry to do, and then I want to call Julie to see if that jerk ever called back. You do what you need to do, and I'll keep busy.

"I probably won't be home for lunch. I'll grab a bite somewhere. I can grab a sandwich and some fries at the coffee shop in Belford."

Cathy waved goodbye as he went out the door with the ledger and his notes in hand. He knew that on a Sunday morning most businesses wouldn't be open, and most of those would stay closed all day. However, this would give him a chance to check out addresses and to see for himself which were still in business. He'd noted that Stanley had visited some stores and shops more frequently than others. He would check those out first.

His first stop was a Cruxton bakery and donut shop that was open, but a young woman was behind the counter. Kevin guessed that Stanley had either kept them supplied with sweeper bags or had stopped for donuts and coffee and written it off as a stop on his sales route. On the same street was the gospel book store, now closed. Lester's repetition of the word evil rang in Kevin's ears, and he put a question mark next to the store's name in his notes.

Having parked his car, he began walking. He was pretty much alone on the sidewalk, and he stopped to peer into windows and read signs. As he was crossing the street, his cell phone rang, and he recognized the incoming call coming from home. "Hi, Cathy. I'm enjoying a leisurely Sunday stroll through the bustling Cruxton business Mecca."

"I thought you might be bored, so I called just to say hello."

After the exchange of goodbyes, Kevin continued his walk. The used car dealer-ship was closed, as was the pet store. The print shop listed in the ledger had apparently moved, and in its place was a used clothing store. It was closed and held no interest. The Starlight Cleaners was gone and the building torn down. The lot was now off-street parking for the adjacent bank. The tentative association with the word steam had apparently fizzled out.

During the short drive to Bedford, Kevin wondered what he would find. Just inside the town was a strip mall that would not have been there in the early 1980's. An address on Edgewood Lane that had not been identified was the Bedford Country Treasurer's office. The garden supply store was adjacent to the feed mill, both of which were on Stanley's list, but both were closed now, too. Kevin put a check mark after the Bedford Farm and Garden Supply store, remembering the coroner's speculation that the bruise from the blunt instrument used to knock Stanley unconscious resembled the shape of a garden trowel. As he drove slowly past the men's clothing store, his attention was drawn to the banner stretching across the display window. For some reason its bold letters proclaiming Summer Sale brought him to a stop in the middle of the street. After having parked, he walked toward the store window, where two manikins stood with frozen stares. Both were dressed in lightweight summer suits, one tan and the other a subtle gray pinstripe. He wondered why he'd never felt the need to buy a suit after buying the one in which he had been married.

He wondered why this attraction now. Sale signs could easily attract Cathy, but he'd always felt immune to their hypnotic spell.

The ties he had were obviously out of style, and the only dress shirts he owned were white. What was he missing? He wondered if Margaret wanted him to buy a new wardrobe with wider ties and colored shirts. He stepped back across the sidewalk to the curb for a fuller view of the lifeless models and their attire, but when he did, he noticed a nine-by-eleven white cardboard sign in the lower right corner of the window. Moving close again, he read Free Alterations, but what caught his eye were the drawings of a pair of scissors and a needle and thread. "Scissors," he said out loud. Back in his car he put two check marks after the clothing store's name.

He was about to pull away from where he had parked when he noticed a sign hanging above a door just up the block.

That door apparently led to a second floor office about the clothing store. He got out of his car and walked closer, so as to be sure he had read it correctly. He hit the auto dial button on his phone and Cathy answered.

"Hon, you know all the clues we have associated with a seamstress or tailor that now seem to somehow fit the men's clothing store's alterations service?"

"Sounds like you've made some new associations, but you're changing you line of thinking. Where are you going in your head?"

"It might not be sewing. Right next to the men's clothing store is a door that leads to offices above it. The shingle hanging over that door is for Simpson and Taylor, Attorneys. Taylor. What if it's a first or last name we need to be tying in with the scissors and stuff?"

"I talked with Julie today, and she had a question we haven't considered. She wondered this: if Margaret knew who the killer was, why didn't she tell Mike when he was investigating the case?"

"Whoa, that is something we've not considered."

"You know Julie. She said if she had never been touched by a man she probably wouldn't know where her erogenous spots were."

"Wait, what the hell does Julie's physical sensitivity have to do with Stanley's murderer?"

"She said if she wanted a man to find the unknown, but was uncertain herself about exactly where it was located, she could only give vague clues and hope he could then discover it on his own."

"Okay, so you're thinking that Margaret is saying that she knows it's someone out there, but all she can do is get us in the vicinity and hope we discover something she doesn't know."

"Yep. Maybe we just have to keep feeling around, and hope that we eventually stumble over the killer. I wonder if the J is for Julie. She's not old enough to be the murderer, but she might have figured out why Margaret is so cryptic."

"Well, no one said this was going to be easy. I'm heading for a coffee break, and I'll think about Julie's role while I have a cinnamon one."

On Stan's route list was the Rainbow Coffee Shop where Kevin had first met Mike. Kevin had saved it for his last stop in Bedford. He was surprised to see that the parking lot was almost full, and he had to wait ten minutes even to get a seat at the counter. When he sat, he was immediately greeted by a waitress other than the one with whom Mike had flirted. He acknowledged that he'd start with coffee. As the woman filled his cup, he impulsively asked, "Where's the redhead who waits on tables?"

"Oh, that's Marie. She used to be fulltime, but now she's a sub."

Kevin concealed his grin as he thought of how Marie had turned on when Mike came across as a dominant male, and she slipped into the submissive role. While he waited to give his order, he reached into his shirt pocket to retrieve his list. He realized that this was the shirt he had worn when visiting Chief Bailey, and that he had not taken the picture of Stan and the unknown Steven out of the pocket. At that point, a cook in the kitchen reached a plate through a window across from where he sat, and called out "Rainbow Founder's Special." Kevin observed that the two cooks visible through the window were obviously both in their sixties.

When the waitress returned, Kevin asked, "What is the Rainbow Founder's Special I heard the cook call out?"

"Oh," she replied, you must mean flounders. The Rainbow Flounders Special, but it's only served on Fridays, so you couldn't have heard it today."

Kevin was going to argue that he heard the cook say something that sound like founders, but this would not be the first time Margaret had manipulated his awareness. "Have the two cooks worked here for long?" he asked.

"Forever. They've both been here since the restaurant opened up in 1977. They both started as waiters."

"Do me a big favor, and I'll leave you a big tip. Show this picture to them, and ask if they recognize either of the two men. This was taken back in 1980."

"I don't have to ask them. There's a picture just like this hanging back in the kitchen. They co-founded this shop, and are affectionately referred to as the two founding S's – Stanley and Steven."

Kevin's mouth hung open. He looked up over the window to the kitchen, and saw a rainbow he had not noticed earlier. Its seven colors, top to bottom, were red, orange, yellow, green, blue, indigo, and violet. "Of course," he said out loud. Then, having composed himself, he asked if she knew the last names of the founders.

"No, but I'll ask the guys in the kitchen." She exited through a swinging door, and within a minute, she reentered, followed by both cooks. Each was wearing a white T-shirt and a white bib apron. One was slender, and the other rotund. The thinner cook was bald, and it appeared that he had shaved off any remaining hair. He wore a gold earring through his left earlobe. The heavier cook had thick, snow-white hair, long and pulled back, all packed inside a black hairnet.

Kevin laid the photograph on the counter. Before he could say anything, the thinner cook picked it up. "Where did you get this picture?" he asked.

"I have a real interest in Stanley's family, and in what had happened to him."

"Are you a cop?" the other cook asked.

"No, but I'm interested in the case, and I'm working with the police."

"Finally," the heavier of the two said. "You're not going to give up, are you?"

"No. I am not going to give up, and there are others now who are helping us to find Stan's killer."

"You don't know how many years we've been waiting for this," the other cook stated.

"Twenty-five," Kevin shot back, "but I'm with a team that's dedicated to finding the murderer."

"Steve will be so happy to hear this," the taller cook said.

"So you do recognize this man with Stanley as a fellow named Steve?"

"Definitely," the two men said in unison.

Kevin had another question he needed to get out of the way. "Mike, the detective who originally investigated the case, has been coming here on a regular basis for twenty-some years. Have you ever talked with him?"

"You need to understand. Back in the seventies and early eighties, the gay community here in Bedford was paranoid as hell. Everyone knew of the police department's anti-gay prejudice."

The taller, thinner cook picked up the story. "We never knew where Mike stood, so we've kept a low profile, which is easy to do when he's out here flirting with Marie, and we're back in the kitchen cooking."

"I can assure you both that Mike is an okay guy, and he's felt terrible for all these years, feeling that he let Stan's parents down and wishing he had had the guts to stand up to the bigoted chief. Get to know him. He's on our side. But, tell me. how can I get in touch with Steven?"

"He's no longer in town, but we both still keep in touch with him."

"He's moved to Florida," the other added.

"Can you give me his name and telephone number?"

The two men looked at each other, and then the slim one said, "It would be better if we got your name and number, and he could then call you."

"He was scared when he left. He said he'd never feel safe coming back to Bedford," the heavier cook added.

"Do you know why?" Kevin asked.

The heavier cook leaned over the counter, put his hand on Kevin's and said, "He'll have to answer that question, dear."

Kevin wrote his name, home number, cell phone number and email address on a napkin and handed it to the thinner man, who winked. "We wish you and Bill all the best."

Kevin was about to ask how they knew about Bill, but he answered his own question and instead asked, "Will I see you both Thursday night?"

Now the two cooks briefly clasped hands. "He's Ted and I'm Larry. We'll be there."

Kevin winked, thanked them, and they headed back into the kitchen. He settled for two cups of coffee and a cinnamon roll as his lunch, left the waitress a big tip and headed for Findley. The hardware store was still in business and still located at the same address written in Stan's sales route ledger. The check mark was a reminder that garden trowels were probably sold there. The Red Bull Meat Market was still in business, and knives as thick as a hunting knife would probably be used there. The meat market also got a check mark. The office supply store and the barber shop – businesses associated with scissors – were still in business.

All of the establishments were closed on this Sunday afternoon, and Kevin was eager to get home and relax. Given that Findley was the furthest from home, he had time to think and wonder. *Was Steven afraid of getting arrested for killing Stanley, and is that why he fled to Florida? Maybe he was just afraid of persecution by the police for just being gay.*

The notion that Steven might be the killer did not receive a high score on Kevin's probability scale, for had Steve been the murderer, he would not have stayed in touch with the two gay cooks. Kevin also downplayed any hope of finding the killer in the garden supply or hardware stores. He saw an even slimmer chance of finding him or her in the meat market.

Her? he mused. *We have not really considered the possibility that the killer could be a her and not a him. If so, what could the motive be? Was Stan fooling around with someone's husband, or maybe her son? Pieces of the puzzle have to start fitting together soon.*

Chapter Eleven

Kevin was feeling that his discussion with the two cooks at the coffee shop had been very productive, and he was pleased they were willing to send his name and phone number to Steve, who had moved to Florida, probably out of fear for his own life.

Driving home, still holding the steering wheel, Kevin crossed fingers on both hands. "Margaret," he said out loud, "all we can do is feel around. You get us headed in the general direction, and we'll find the hot spots."

He was approaching the edge of Cruxton when his cell phone rang in the way it identified a call from home. "Hi, hon."

"Are you going to be home soon?"

"I'm just turning onto Maple, so I should be there in about fifteen minutes. Anything happening?"

"Nah, just missing you."

"I'll fill you in on my surprises when I get there. Right now all I can think of is food. I'm starved. What's for dinner?"

"You'll have to fend for yourself. We've been pigging out lately, so I'm having a low-cal frozen dinner tonight. My shorts were a bit snug this morning."

"Hey, I'll have one of those dinners too, and some moose tracks ice cream for dessert."

He made good time getting through town, for at every intersection the traffic light was green. Cathy would usually greet him at the door, but she was on the phone talking with Julie. As he walked into the living room, he saw his wife sitting on the couch, and for a brief moment, he beheld the semi-transparent figure of a young woman standing behind her. Margaret was no doubt eavesdropping on the girl talk.

Just as Cathy hung up the phone, Kevin spoke. "Julie. Her name reminds me that we've not really talked much about the gender of the one who murdered Stan. As we had said before, that initial J could be for Janet or Jessie or dozens of other female names, and I'm wondering if we need to think seriously about that possibility."

"Well, the only J who's guilty of anything I can think of is Julie, and she's only guilty of picking up another man."

"That reminds me of something funny that happened in the coffee shop where Mike had been hitting on a waitress for years, but without ever scoring. I think I told you how he got ticked off and yelled something like 'Back off, lady,' and that show of dominance turned her on. So, she saw him as Dom and she became his submissive. Well, today, when I asked about her, another waitress said she only works part time and described her as a sub."

Cathy showed no reaction.

Mike shrugged. "I guess you'd have to have been there. Anyway, the most important thing I learned today is that Stanley and the Steven in the pictures were not only lovers, they were also the cofounders of the Rainbow Coffee Shop in Bedford. I didn't notice when I was first there, but the rainbow on their sign and the one on a wall in the shop are the same colors of the Gay Pride flag hanging on the wall of the bar in Findley."

"Well, that's certainly interesting, but how does it help?"

"Patience, girl, patience. The good part is that the two cooks have been there since the beginning, and even though the ownership has changed, they've stayed in touch with Steven. He apparently became scared about something and fled to Florida."

"What do you think? Scared by Margaret? Scared of being arrested?"

"Or scared of also being murdered, or maybe just of being harassed by the police. The cooks said the gays in Bedford had been very paranoid about the cops. They took my name and information, saying they'd get it to Steven. They seemed confident he'd call."

"That was kind of them."

"Well, I really think Ted and Larry are genuinely eager to see this case solved."

"First name basis?"

"Yep, and I'll probably see them again on Thursday night."

"At the gay bar?"

"Uh-huh. Are you worried about the competition?"

"No way am I worried. I know you'll come home to me. But, I can't help wondering why Mike didn't tell us about Stan and Steve's connection with the coffee shop. You told me Mike hangs out there a lot."

"That's a question I plan to ask him, but right now I'm thinking frozen dinner."

"Let's eat."

* * * * *

After dinner, they curled up on the couch, exchanging foot massages while watching a scary TV movie about a haunted house.

"I'm surely glad our ghost is a friendly one," Cathy said as the movie ended and the credits began to roll.

"Well, the former Bedford Chief of Police knows a very different side of our Margaret."

"Do you think Nick will find out anything more about the old guy's release?"

"I don't know, and I also don't know if I'll ever hear from Steven."

"I guess that'll all have to wait. It's bedtime now."

* * * * *

Kevin's snoring woke Cathy in the morning, although she had slept well. Feeling wide awake and ready to start her day, she tried slipping quietly out of bed, but Kevin's eyes popped open. "Holy cow," were the first words out of his mouth. He sat straight up in bed.

"What's that about?"

"I just had the strangest dream. In it I was making out with a very sexy woman and getting all excited. I'll tell you more, but right now I need to go to the bathroom." He walked into the bathroom and from there he called out, "I've got to finish telling you about my weird dream."

Cathy walked into the bathroom. "So, tell me about the dream."

"As I said, I was making out, my eyes were closed and I was getting all excited. Then when I opened my eyes, I discovered that this wasn't a woman. It was a man. It shocked the hell out of me and woke me."

"Oh, my God, Kevin. Are you turning gay?"

"Certainly not that I'm aware of, Cathy. In the dream I was surprised and backed away quickly. I felt no hostility toward the man, but no attraction either."

"Then I'll fix you breakfast."

As she turned, he smacked her lightly on her bottom,

"Just remember, I'm full time, not your sub."

"Yes, mistress." Kevin replied.

* * * * *

After breakfast, Cathy showered and started the laundry as Kevin nursed a cup of coffee while watching the TV coverage of national news. He was about to get up to refill his cup when the phone rang. The caller proved to be Chief Harris.

"Good morning, Nick. What's new with the Bedford Police Chief this morning?"

"I just wanted to check in with you. I talked with the hospital superintendent again, but there really isn't any new information. He just said again how helpless he felt when Judith, Lester's daughter, insisted on his release."

"Judith? Lester's daughter's name is Judith?"

"Yeah. I thought he had a son, but I must've been wrong."

"Or the son had a sex change operation."

"Now that would have been enough to drive Lester crazy. He was known for his hatred of gays and the gender-benders."

"Hmmm, all very interesting. Anything else?"

"Well, just this, and it fits. The super said that as the attendants were helping to get Lester into the daughter's car, he kept calling them gay and evil, and that kind of stuff. Margaret must have gotten in the car with them, because the super also said that Lester, as they drove away, was still yelling for her to stop screaming."

"Thanks for the information, Nick. I'll share this with Cathy." After hanging up, he walked into the laundry room, where she was sorting the whites from the colored clothes.

"Who was on the phone?"

"It was Chief Harris. I don't know if his information is helpful or just confusing. First of all, Lester's daughter's name could fit the mysterious initial J in Margaret's diary. Her name is Judith. At least, now, the woman's name is Judith," he repeated, "but she might not have been born female. Nick thought Lester's kid was a man. So, the question is, is Judith a transsexual, and if so, how does that fit?"

"And it could also be related to the maple syrup image of the scissors. Male parts were snipped off."

"Margaret's entry about things becoming unstitched could have been her naïve way of describing the surgical creation of female accessories."

"Now, I think that's a bit of a stretch, Kev."

"And the scissors also showed up on a sign in the window of the men's clothing store in Bedford, but does that mean we need to look for a man or a man who's been clipped? I'm confused."

"Well, what about the vortex in the toilet swirling in the wrong direction? We thought we knew what she was telling us, but now I wonder."

"And the announcement of the gallery's art show – it went blank. What do we need to cut out, flush away or wipe clean?"

"Hey, let's try not to get too carried away, Kevin. I don't think we understand all the clues or have all the facts."

"Julie's metaphor about having to search the vicinity hoping to find the goodies does make sense. I would think that if Margaret knew the name of the killer, she would have sent us an email. Right now I'm not sure if we understand *any* of the clues."

"Well, Lester's prejudice against gays and his perception of them as evil was confirmed," Cathy stated.

"And the good news is that the screaming Margaret has gone with the SOB."

"Give him hell, girl. Give him hell!"

A semi-transparent Margaret Ann, fist raised in the air, drifted across the room and vanished into the wall.

Kevin and Cathy spontaneously raised their fists too, and then burst out laughing.

"Moving on now," he said, and then kissed Cathy on the tip of her nose. "I need to talk with Mike, but he might not be up yet. I've got to know why he didn't tell us about Stan's co-founding the coffee shop with Steve. But first I need to refill my cup." Kevin declared, raising it into the air.

"I'm with you," Cathy said, grabbing her empty coffee cup from atop the washing machine and lifting it also into the air, matching his gesture of determination.

As they refilled their cups in the kitchen, the phone rang again. *It's pretty early,* passed through Kevin's mind as he reached to answer the strange voice that said, "Hello." He hesitated and then replied, "Yes, this is Kevin Riley." There was another pause as he listened.

"My name is Steve. I'm a longtime friend of Stanley, and I'm calling you from Florida."

"Oh, my God, Steven. I was afraid you wouldn't call. Can I put you on hold, so my wife and I can get to the phone with a speaker?" Cathy was already on her way to the living room when Steve agreed. Kevin said, "Thanks. I'll only be a minute." He ran to the living room and pushed the phone's speaker button.

"My wife Cathy is here with me now, so we'll both be able to hear you."

"Ted called me last night and told me of your conversation in the coffee shop, but I'm not clear on your connection with Stan."

"Call it accident or fate, but I work as a mover. Stan's mother, Margaret, died not too long ago, and I moved her stuff from her house."

Steven interrupted. "I'm sorry to hear she's gone. I really liked her, and she was so good to Stan and me. I felt like a part of the family."

"Well, she's gone, but she's not *really* gone. Just bear with me, please, because this gets pretty weird. I was somehow drawn to Margaret's diary and a portrait of her and her husband John, who died about nine years before she did, and a collection of family pictures. That's where I found pictures of you and Stan."

"You took those things from her home?"

"Plus her wedding dress, and Stan's sales route ledger."

"Yeah, he ended up selling vacuum sweepers after we sold the coffee shop in 1980. But I'm wondering why you took these things?"

"Because they would have been destroyed or sold at an auction, and something told me I had to take them. I just had this really strong urge to protect and preserve some precious memories."

"Something told you?"

"Okay, here's the weird part. I saw Margaret Ann's ghost. I know that sounds crazy, but she has led Cathy and me to the discovery of the tragic circumstances of her son's death. We've come to believe that she's stuck here because the one who took Stan's life hasn't been found and punished. I know this will sound strange, but I think I was somehow picked to solve this case."

There was silence on the phone for several moments. Finally, Steve whispered, "You are the man."

"What?"

"I said, you *are* the man. After I fled to Florida, fearing for my own life, I received a letter from Stan's mother. In it she said that none of us will rest until the one who stole Stanley from us is brought to justice. Then she added this statement: when you hear his voice, you'll know it is the man who will avenge our loss. I have saved that letter for twenty-five years, and I've been waiting. It's *your* voice I have been waiting for."

"Add this to our collection of unexplainable events. The guy who was the police chief when you were in Bedford has been incoherent and bizarre for well over twenty years. But he looked right into my eyes with full awareness, and said the same words: 'You are the man.'"

"We believe it, and both Kevin and I have seen Margaret," Cathy said.

"Cathy is on the team, and so is the present police chief, a gay police officer and a gay friend of mine named Bill."

"Yeah, Ted mentioned you and Bill. Are you bi?"

"No, Steve, I have to come out to you as being pretty straight. But I feel I need to make contact with anyone at the bar who remembers Stan. I'm still digging for information, and Bill is helping me fit into the bar scene by pretending to be my partner, and a bear at that."

"I wish I could help too. I sincerely grieve the deaths of both Margaret and John. They were good people: the kind of fantastic parents every gay or lesbian would hope for. Now, add this to your facts and questions. Stan and I were off-and-on-again lovers, but we were always the very best of friends. He dated another guy named Steve: a black artist, whom the police questioned, but he was innocent. I drifted in and out while he played around with Steve Number Two, as we named him. But, then Stan got himself involved with another man who was possessive as hell. He had Stan so frightened that he wouldn't tell me who this guy was – not his name or where he lived. The man had forbidden it, insisting on total secrecy, and he kept a very close eye on Stan."

Steve hesitated, and from Cathy came an audible "Phew."

"I think I know where this is going," Kevin said.

Steve continued. "Yeah, you can probably see it coming. Stan and I had a long history and, I think, an undying love and attraction for each other. It had been a while since we talked, and he and I started talking on the phone. We even exchanged a few letters. We planned to meet, but I waited for him all night in the motel room: our usual rendezvous spot. In the morning I learned the tragic news that Stan had been attacked and had been taken unconscious in the hospital. I felt I had to go and see him, but later that day, when I started out to my car, I found a note tacked to my door. All it said was, *He's mine, and now you will pay for your evil.*"

The audible "Phew" this time was from Kevin.

"God almighty," was Cathy's reaction.

"It's crazy," Steve continued, "but my first thought was that someone thought that I killed Stan. God knows I loved that man and would never have caused him harm. Then I realized that the note was from the controlling bastard whom Stan had been seeing, because after Stan died, there was another note saying *It was your fault. You brought the evil and made me do it and I'll get you for that.* I remember those notes as if I had read them yesterday. I felt helpless and scared, and I ran."

"So that's why you fled," Kevin said. "I can certainly understand."

"I'll email you my full name, address and phone number. Please, Kevin, keep me posted, and if I'm needed there to testify or anything, please don't hesitate to call."

"Thanks, Steve. You've filled in some blanks, but I have one last really strange question. Do you have any reason to believe that the possessive guy Stan had been seeing was in fact a transsexual who could now be a woman?"

Steve laughed.

"Okay, we'll cross that off."

"I have a question for you, Steve, but I think I can guess the answer." Cathy hesitated, and then continued. "Did you or any of the gay men you knew here ever have any run-ins with the Bedford police?"

"Oh, my, we were harassed continually by the police, but everyone knew that started at the top. Chief Bailey was a hateful bigot. I can remember him going on and on about the evils of the homosexual lifestyle. We also worried about the detective who was leading the investigation. We just never knew where he stood."

Cathy was the one to respond. "I want to assure you that Mike, the detective who is now retired, is on our side all the way. He has obsessed for decades about his failure to stand up to the chief and to solve the case. He's working with us now to uncover facts and to get the case reopened. The present chief of police is also on our team."

"You'll be happy to know also," Kevin said, "that Margaret's ghost has a not-so-nice side. She's been haunting Lester for well over twenty years and has driven him crazy."

"Good for her," Steve commented.

"Good for all of us," Cathy added.

After the call ended, the Rileys sat in silence for a few minutes. Finally, Kevin spoke. "That was productive. I think we're starting to focus in a little better now. We have to find out who that secretive, controlling man was. It seems he's now our prime suspect."

Chapter Twelve

"It might be okay to focus on identifying the domineering possessive man Stan was in a relationship, but what about Judith, the former chief's daughter. Why did she spring him from the mental institution when she learned that you had shown him a picture of Stan and Steve?" Cathy asked.

"Maybe that's what Margaret was telling me in that dream. Originally, I took an interest in Judith because of the J initial, and in my mind that made her a possible suspect. But Margaret knew the killer was a male, biologically or surgically, so I had to change my thinking and look for someone masculine." He turned in the direction where they had last seen the apparition. "But please, Margaret, the next time you have me in a dream making out with a beautiful woman, let me make love to her before turning her into a man."

Cathy also looked in that direction. "And if the man turns out to be handsome as Kev said he was, let *me* dream about him tonight." She then turned to her husband who was grinning from ear to ear.

Margaret giggled.

Buster ran from the bedroom as if being chased by a pack of dogs. He leaped up onto the kitchen counter and in the process knocked over a wooden fruit bowl. On hearing it hit the floor, Kevin and Cathy ran into the kitchen. The bowl had only held apples, oranges and pears.

"So what's the message?" Kevin asked as he helped pick up the fruit that had rolled in all directions.

"I think the message is that everything happening now does not necessarily contain a hidden message from Margaret. Sometimes cats just have bad dreams and knock things over."

"Wait. Oranges, Florida, Steve."

"Let it go, Kev. Buster was just being a cat, not a messenger."

When the fruit had all been picked up and Kevin was about to get off his hand and knees, he noticed something glisten in a patch of sunlight just in front of the refrigerator. Having crawled to it, he asked, "Were you sewing in here?"

"No, I only sew in my sewing area of the office. Why?"

"Because there's a needle over here on the floor."

"I have no idea how it could have gotten in here. It's not likely that Buster carried it in."

"Nonetheless, here it is," Kevin said, pointing to it.

"Coming unstitched. She wrote that things were coming unstitched." Cathy crawled over to where Kevin was, and they both sat up and leaned back against a cupboard door. "And the maple syrup scissors."

"And there was the needle and thread, along with scissors, on the sign in the men's clothing store window. Now the iron takes on new meaning. I thought it was just the concept of something hot leading me to the hot water radiators in Margaret's house."

"We're back to considering either a tailor by occupation, or someone whose last name is Taylor. There was a tailor shop on Stan's sales route, right?"

"Yes, and it was in Bedford, but I checked the address out on Sunday and found out it's now a greetings card store."

"Think Margaret is losing her marbles and purposefully sending us confusing messages."

Buster let out a loud screech, pounced into Cathy's lap and bounced out again. His behavior scared her more than it harmed her, but she got the message. "Sorry, Margaret. I was only kidding. We really are trying to understand how the needle fits with other clues, and we think we've on the brink of making sense out all you've been trying to tell us."

"A very secretive and possessive man whose name, first or last, starts with a J and who possibly owned a tailor shop. Now let's hope that I can fill in more missing pieces on Thursday."

"And I promise to behave, Margaret, and you're forgiven, Buster," Cathy said to the cat who was nudging her with his head to get her attention.

"Don't you dare," Kevin said to his wife as he laid his head in her lap. "Don't you dare behave."

"I'll be naughty if you promise to barbeque some chicken for dinner. I have some in the freezer that we can put out to thaw."

"Let's get through breakfast first."

During breakfast, Kevin and Cathy talked of Stan and Steve's founding of the coffee shop and how after three years they sold it, but stayed in touch with the two gay waiters who eventually became cooks. "Time is fascinating, isn't it?" Kevin asked. "It goes by so fast, and so many things change."

"It's hard to imagine what it must have been like being gay in Bedford back in the seventies."

"I guess if anything good has come out of this tragedy, it was the ending of Chief Bailey's control of the police department."

"Yes," Cathy added, "and it's wonderful that Chief Harris is so open-minded."

"And so willing to help," Kevin added to that.

"You mentioned change, but think of what hasn't changed. We are seeing the endless love of a woman for her husband and child, and the endless love Steven still feels for Stan."

Kevin took Cathy in his arms. "You are a good woman, and I love you."

After finishing his coffee he invited Cathy into the living room so that he could call Mike and she could listen on the speaker. She followed him, and they sat together on the couch. Kevin entered the stored number with the auto-dial button.

"Hello," Mike answered on the third ring.

"I hope we didn't wake you up this morning."

"Nope. I've been up for a while, and have been sitting here thinking about a dream I had last night."

"We think Margaret influences our dreams," Cathy said. "She might have sent you a message, so tell us yours."

"I'm not sure if it did have any meaning, and if so, I sure as hell can't figure it out. Anyway, it was pretty short. I was in the coffee shop, but it was dark and I felt all alone. Marie, the waitress, came out of the kitchen and kicked the old juke box, and the damn thing started playing. It was just piano music, but I recognized it as the old piece titled *Endless Love.*"

Cathy said nothing, but reached over and took hold of Kevin's hand.

Mike continued with his dream. "The two cooks came out and started dancing, and then Marie told me to dance with them. I did, and it somehow felt right – as if it were something I've needed to do for a long time. Crazy, right?"

"Maybe crazier than you think, or else clear as a bell." Kevin replied. "We believe that Margaret not only sends us messages in dreams, but can also influence the words we hear or say. You said the cooks came out, and that could be interpreted as coming out with their gayness. Did you know they were gay?"

"No. I never really thought of it. I guess in the dream they came out to me."

"Well, they're gay and they've been dancing together for a lot of years."

Cathy then spoke. "In the dream it seemed like Marie, but I think it was Margaret who told you to join with Ted and Larry."

"Explain that to me. She didn't, doesn't, want me to be gay, does she?" He sounded worried.

"No, I meant join as a comrade – discovering their love of Stanley and you opening up and allowing them to understand your commitment to solving this case. We're all on the same team, dancing to the same tune, gay and straight."

"I started going there when I first started my investigation. I'd driven by the shop so many times, but never stopped. For some reason I quickly developed the feeling of some kind of connection to the place, but assumed it was because I had the hots for Marie. I guess I've really been in the dark."

"Did you know, Mike, that Stanley was the co-founder of the shop in 1977, and co-owned it until 1980 with the unidentified Steven in the Morgan family pictures?"

"Holy cow, that's news to me. Wow! How did I not know that? In 1983, when Stan was murdered, he was selling vacuum sweepers. I knew nothing about his previous employment or business ventures before that. I never thought to ask. Wow, you two are better detectives than I ever was! You even know the names of the cooks. During all the years I've been going there and checking out that redhead's bottom, I never once heard their names of the guys in the kitchen, and I sure as hell never knew who started the place."

"It's not all your fault," Kevin said. Stan and Steve had already sold the place when you came on the scene, and the cooks were avoiding you. Somehow, and it's not your fault, you got lumped in with all the paranoia associated with the Bedford police. They didn't know if you were trying to solve the case or sabotage it."

"Oh, my God. If only I'd have known, I would have talked with them. I don't know if that would have helped us solve the case, but at least we would have been communicating all these years. We do have a common goal."

"Yes, they have an undying love for Steven, Stanley and Stan's family, and share with us the desire to find closure," Kevin said. Sighing, he added, "This has gone on much too long."

"So Ted and Larry now know we are on the same side. Good. The lights came on, and I saw things I have not seen before. The music stated playing and I discovered there are others dancing to the same music I've been dancing to, but all alone, ever since Stanley died."

"Wow," Cathy said.

"Wow indeed," Kevin added, then repeating himself, he breathed, "This has gone on much too long."

"I am so very glad we talked this morning," Mike said. "I'm going to have lunch at the coffee shop today. I want to meet Ted and Larry. Will you two join me?"

"Eleven-thirty?" Cathy wondered.

"It's a date," Mike confirmed. "See you there."

After the goodbyes were exchanged, Kevin and Cathy snuggled on the couch. Their hugs and kiss were important.

"Endless love," Cathy whispered.

* * * * *

The morning passed slowly, with each spouse frequently checking the clock. Both were cleaned up and ready to go well before the time they would need to leave to be at the coffee by eleven-thirty. "It's a beautiful day. Let's drive to the park and walk that two-mile wooded trail," Cathy suggested. "Maybe it will help us unwind."

"Great idea. We have plenty of time and I can use the exercise."

The drive to the park, the walk among the trees, their sitting on a shaded bench to listen to the birds, and then the drive to Bedford filled the time gap. They arrived to see Mike getting out of his car. Having greeted him at the door, they walked into the Rainbow Coffee Shop together. There were tables available, and when not crowded, customers would typically seat themselves.

Mike led the way, saying, "We'll sit at that table near the juke box."

"I'll ask the waitress to tell the cooks we're here," Kevin said, but before a waitress arrived, Ted and Larry came out of the kitchen. Each introduced himself to Mike and to Cathy. A bit of small talk followed, including promises of spending more time together, but the cooks excused themselves when the waitress arrived.

"We've got some food on the stove we'd better check," Larry said.

The smiles, more than the words, spoke of a newfound comfort and understanding. It would be a slow dance, but now everyone was in step.

"What can I get you to drink?" the petite blonde waitress asked.

"I'll have a diet Coke," a woman's voice declared, and when the three looked up they saw a slightly overweight redheaded woman in her fifties.

"Marie," Mike said, pleasant surprise evident in his voice.

"Can I join you?" she asked.

Mike looked around.

Kevin stood. "Please sit. You're more than welcome."

Rising, Mike pushed the chair under the sub, who was not now dressed in the pink bib skirt and lacey blouse forming the coffee shop uniform. She wore a plain white, low-cut cotton blouse, a black skirt and fishnet hose. Before he sat back down, without offering an explanation, he pulled a pair of handcuffs out of a back pocket and laid them on the table.

Under the table, Cathy squeezed her husband's knee and introduced herself to Marie, adding "I'm Kevin's mistress."

Marie smiled. "I'm Mike's."

Lunch was fun. They laughed and teased, grew sentimental and raunchy, and promised to meet again in a week at a hot tub party Marie would be throwing. "Clothing optional," she added with a wink.

"Bad girl," Mike growled, and Marie submissively lowered her eyes.

He catches on fast, Kevin thought to himself and he squeezed Cathy's knee.

* * * * *

On Tuesday, Kevin worked all day moving an older couple from their home into a condo across town. On Wednesday morning, he and Bill spent the morning helping another two-man crew move office furniture and files from one wing to a newly-renovated wing at the other end of the building. He was home in time to have lunch with Cathy.

"What are your plans for this afternoon?" she asked.

"I want to drive to Bedford to see if I can learn anything about the tailor shop that's no longer there. Somebody might remember it and the tailor."

"Good luck. I'll spend the time working on some new songs to teach the kids this fall. You have fun."

Kevin held his sexy wife. She looked so pretty with her long brown hair pulled back and tied. He loved this woman, and loved having her home during the summer. He'd miss her once school started up again, but this would give him time to work on his writing.

They kissed. Kevin promised to be home for dinner, and they said goodbye.

* * * * *

Kevin parked in front of the Bedford's Forever Yours Card Shop, and sat looking at it as though he could go back in time and see the tailor shop. However, the card shop stayed the card shop. Shrugging, he got out of his car and entered the store. A short series of chimes sounded to announce his entry.

"How long has this store been here?" he asked the middle-aged woman behind the trinket-filled counter.

"I'm not too sure. I've worked here since '98, and I recall the woman I replaced saying she'd been here for five years. I remember thinking that was a long time, but I've now been here twice as long."

"Did that woman start working here when the shop first opened?"

"I think she might've, or shortly after it opened."

"That puts the opening back, then, to the early nineteen nineties."

"Something like that, I guess. Can I help you find a card?"

"No, I'm just curious. My mother talked about coming to a tailor shop here, and I was just wondering what had happened to it."

"I remember it too, and now that I think of it, that shop closed sometime in the mid-eighties. I remember walking by it on my way to high school. It was still here when I graduated in 1980 and moved. I came back to Bedford in '85 and the tailor shop was closed. The building was empty for a year or two. I remember the kids saying the building was jinxed."

"Did you ever know the tailor?"

"I saw him a couple of times, but I never really knew him."

"But the tailor was a man?"

"Oh, yes." The salesclerk acted as if she needed to straighten up the counter. "Are you sure there's not something I can help you find?"

"No, but you've been helpful." He turned and was about to leave, but then turned back with a question that just occurred to him. "The woman who worked here before you — is she still around?"

"No, I heard that she died about three years ago."

Kevin thanked her again and drove the short distance to the coffee shop. It was not crowded, and he sat on a stool at the counter. He asked the waitress for a cup of coffee and then asked if he could talk with either Ted or Larry.

As she was filling his cup, she called through the window into the kitchen. Ted came through the swinging doors wiping his hands on his apron.

"Hi, Kevin. What brings you to Bedford?"

"I wanted to check on the tailor who had the shop over on Chestnut. Did you know him at all?"

"Not really. He was very secretive. I hardly ever saw him at the bar, but he has been a regular at the yearly memorial gatherings held for Stan."

"So he's gay?"

"I don't think he's really out with it, but yeah, I'm pretty sure he is. Now, you know, at the bar we don't discriminate against straights. But I really do think this guy is gay."

"Did you ever see him with Stan?"

"I never saw him with anyone. As I said, he's a pretty private guy."

"You don't know his name, then?"

"No, but I'll bet the bartender does."

"Thanks. I'll ask Bruce when I'm there tomorrow night."

"You and Bill?"

"Yeah, I'll be with Bill."

Ted headed back to the kitchen and Kevin finished his coffee. He was eager to get home to see Cathy, who had spent the day preparing lessons plans for when school started again.

After greeting each other with hugs and kisses, Kevin asked about her day.

"Nothing new here. No phone calls, no failed romance reports from Julie and no visits from our friendly ghost. How was your day?"

"We might be onto something with the idea of a gay tailor playing some key role in all of this. I'm hoping to learn his identity tomorrow night. He's described as a very private and secretive guy, but he's been showing up regularly for those annual gatherings at the bar."

"You mean when the neon beer sign goes off for a minute?"

"Yeah, when Stan's old friends get together to remember him. I understand the number has dwindled to about six or eight, and when you think about it, that's pretty remarkable after twenty-five years. The bartender should know all their names."

"We can only hope someone knows something we don't," Cathy said. "We seem to be stuck."

Buster's meow seemed to say he shared their frustration.

Chapter Thirteen

"Is anything happening tonight?" Cathy Riley asked her husband.

"Nope." Kevin replied. "I thought I'd catch the evening news, and then I want to sit at the computer and see if I can come up with some ideas for a plot. I'm still determined to write a novel that will interest a publisher, but I'm really not sure where to begin."

"I think you're a natural for writing a hot romance – not too hot and not too romantic."

"I've not been able to find that balance. I just need to feel inspired. It'll probably come to me."

"Ah, the elusive muse."

It was a quiet evening. Kevin sat looking at a blank computer monitor while Cathy worked on a five-hundred-piece puzzle spread out over the kitchen table. By eight o'clock, they were both ready to sit and watch TV.

Wednesday ended quietly, but Thursday started with a bang. Literally. At seven in the morning someone banged on their front door. Pulling on a sweatshirt and pair of sweatpants, Kevin went to see who was out there so early. He knew it wasn't likely to be any of the other drivers or anyone else from work, as his job for that day was not to start until eleven. He unlocked the door, but kept the chain lock hooked. Cautiously, he opened the door, just enough to peer out through the crack. It was Lester Bailey and he looked frantic.

"What do you want?" Kevin yelled through the narrow opening.

"You can stop her. You're the only one who can stop the screaming! You've got to help me! Make her stop!"

"I can't help you. Go away. I can't make her stop."

"Please, you're the man. You can stop her. Make her stop screaming."

"Go away, or I'll call the police." He was about to close and lock the door when he heard a woman's voice from outside.

"Come on, Father, let's go home. You shouldn't be here."

Kevin opened the door to find a slightly overweight woman with dyed black hair. She seemed to be in her fifties. She was pulling on Lester's shirtsleeve. "Sorry about this," she said. "I don't know how he ever got here."

"But he can stop the evil. He's the one. He's the man who can make it all stop."

"Please, Father, come on now. We need to go home."

"Are you Judith?" Kevin asked.

"Yes, I'm Lester's daughter. I'm sorry my dad bothered you. I guess he's going to be a bit harder to manage than I anticipated."

"Aren't there any others in the family who can help?" Kevin asked, digging for information.

Judith hesitated and then responded without giving a direct answer to the question. "I'll be able to manage alone. It just means I have to keep a closer eye on him." She tugged a bit harder on her father's sleeve.

Reluctantly, Lester followed her toward her car, but he continued his ranting. "He has to stop the screaming. He can do it. He's the one. He's got to make the evil stop and end the screaming!"

Kevin stood on the front porch watching Judith coax her father into her car. Just as the woman attempted to fasten her father's seatbelt, Cathy's voice came from inside the house. "What the hell was that all about?"

He turned to see her peering around the half-closed door.

"That was Judith, the woman I had thought started out as a man. She's Lester's daughter: the one who sprang him from the mental hospital."

"But what were they doing here?"

"Somehow Lester got here on his own. There's an early morning bus that comes in from Bedford, but he would have had to walk several blocks. Judith somehow knew where he would be, and came and got him."

"They had our address. Why would they have our address?"

"I have no idea, but the reason she took him out of the hospital was to keep me away from him. She must see me as some kind of a threat."

"The crazies are coming out of the closet."

"That reminds me. Did I tell you that Ted, the cook, described the tailor as having a revolving door on his closet? The guy is apparently gay, but not real open about it."

"When you were in the card store asking about the tailor shop that had once been there, did you ask around in any of the surrounding businesses? I mean, maybe someone knew the tailor better, or knows what's become of him."

"I didn't check around and probably won't have time to go back today. I'll be in Bedford meeting with the gay cop Bud, Mike and Chief Nick, to bring them up to date and find out if they've learned anything new."

"Then I'll ride along. You can drop me off along that strip where most of the shops are located, and I'll just wander around asking questions."

"Great idea, that of riding along and cruising the shops."

"Okay, but let's start with breakfast. Then I want to call Julie and find out what's new in her love life."

"And I'll spend part of this morning cleaning out the back of my truck. Tomorrow I'll need to be up and out early. We're moving a family from up north into town.

"Is Bill helping you on that job?"

"Yeah, and tonight he and I will hit the gay bar tonight. We can't stay too late or drink too much, given the time I'll need to be getting up in the morning."

While Bill was cleaning out his truck Cathy practiced the piano accompaniment for songs she would be teaching the kids in the fall.

Once he had his truck ready ot go, Kevin called Bill, to double-check their meeting time and to remind him of their early morning responsibilities. He had time before lunch to sit at his computer and try again to think of a plot for his unwritten novel. However, once again he failed to come up with any place to begin.

After lunch, Cathy and Kevin headed for the adjacent town of Bedford. When Kevin noticed that she was checking to be sure she had her credit cards, he figured this was more than a fact-finding mission. "Maybe I should have brought the truck," he teased.

"Smart ass," she replied. "You do what you need to do, and I'll do what I need to do."

He dropped her off in front of a jewelry store – her choice – and then headed to the police station. Mike and the chief were waiting for him.

Kevin told of Lester showing up at his door, and how Judith came and got him.

"I hadn't known he had a daughter," Mike said. "I was thinking it was a son."

"I learned about his daughter from the hospital superintendent, when he told me about her demands to take her father home." Nick, the police chief, shook his head. "I never did know much about Lester's family. I took his job when he went crazy, and I focused my attention on getting some organization back into the department."

Kevin told Nick about the cooks having identified the Steven who was in a number of photos with Stan. "Steve and Stan were the co-founders of the Rainbow Coffee Shop, and I think that's why Mike felt a connection with the place. There he was, drinking coffee, ogling the waitress and the whole time he was in the dark about the shop's beginning or the cooks association with Stan."

"So, you learned the full name of the co-founder. Does he hold any significance in this case?" Bud asked.

"Just as a wonderful source of information. I had a long telephone conversation with Steven and learned that Stan had become involved with an unknown and very possessive lover. Steve believed that man threatened his life, and he fled to Florida. Obviously, that mystery lover is of profound interest."

"Any idea how we can find this guy?" the Chief asked.

"I'm optimistic about learning the identity of this man from the bartender in Findley. If we discover that this guy is or was a tailor with a first or last name starting with J, a lot of puzzle pieces would fall into place."

"In light of what you've learned," Chief Harris said, "my information seems pretty insignificant. I've learned that back in

1983, that Steven fellow filed a complaint against an unknown individual who made a couple of death threats, so that confirms his story. Unfortunately, it seems that there was no immediate way to identify the one making the threats, so no action was ever taken. The report identifies both the complaint and the perpetrator as homosexuals, and the anti-gay bias of the former police brass is well known. That makes me wonder if any effort to follow up was even made."

"And I've found something that further supports that bias and takes it right to the top," Mike said. "I talked to one of the guards at the county jail about the case, because he'd mentioned that his father had been on the force and had been responsible for the records room back when Lester Bailey was chief. Two days later, the guy called me. He recalled his father's mention of burying a case and he remembered looking through some notes he had found in his dad's desk after his father had died. He found the note Chief Harris now has, documenting how the then Chief Bailey told Dad he had to order the case closed because the parties involved were evil."

"He was ranting and raving about evil on my porch this morning," Kevin said.

Mike continued, "Evil, Kevin. Even back then, Lester was seeing evil, and that evil was homosexuality. The father's note went on to say that the chief had also ordered him to prevent me from having access to the autopsy report or the case file. It was this officer who then changed the name on the folder, but in the note he talked of pressure from the chief to do so and his own guilt for having caved in."

"Phew." Kevin shook his head in amazement that this note had finally come to light. "It's no wonder Margaret Ann has been screaming at Lester. As we suspected, he stopped the investigation, had evidence concealed and kept you from doing your job, Mike."

"That narrow-minded bigot," Chief Harris added. "I think my predecessor got off pretty easy."

"I'm not so sure how easy it's been toward the end," Mike state. "He's spent a fair amount of time locked up in hell with a screaming ghost."

"Seems she couldn't get to him while she was alive," Bud said, "but she seems to have made up for it after she died."

Kevin's cell phone rang, and he recognized Cathy's cell number on the caller ID. "Hi, hon, we're just finishing up here. Are you ready for me to pick you up?" he asked.

"The dress store's having a sale, so give me another half hour. I wanted to tell you, though, that I've talked with two shop owners who remember Stan and Steven opening the coffee shop. They spoke highly of them. A couple also remember Stan as the vacuum sweeper salesman, but only the old greeter at the door of the discount store could recall the tailor and described him as aloof. But the interesting thing is this, he thinks that after the tailor shop closed, the tailor went to work at the men's store."

"Did you check that out?"

"No. It feels as if we might be getting close, and I don't want to screw things up."

"Good. I'm going to ask Mike to check that out."

After Kevin said goodbye, Mike asked, "What's up?"

Kevin filled the two men in on what Cathy reported, and they both agreed that at this point someone from the department should be involved.

"Let's plan to move tomorrow," the chief advised. "I'll also have Lester picked up, although it doesn't sound as if we'll get much from him."

"Maybe this'll give me a chance to find out more tonight at the bar. I'll call my office and tell them I have a family emergency and can't do that moving job. I'll be free all day tomorrow," Kevin added.

"If you can be here at eight in the morning, we'll see what we can pull together," the chief stated.

"Mind if I bring my wife?"

"Cathy is more than welcome," the chief responded.

"She's part of the team," Mike added.

The men all shook hands. The chief went back to work, Mike went to the coffee shop, and Kevin drove to the dress shop where he met his package-laden wife.

Once home, while Cathy pulled labels off of skirts and blouses, Kevin called into work and reported his need to tend to pressing family matters. He then called Bill, both to confirm their date and to tell him his reasons for taking Friday off.

"I'm calling in sick," Bill said. "If something's coming down tomorrow, there's no way I'm going to be off loading furniture."

"That's great, Bill. You're a member of the team, and you should be there."

After hanging up, Kevin went into the bedroom, where Cathy stood, hanging up her new clothes. He told her of his conversation with Bill, and she agreed that the team should get together, regardless of how the day might unfold.

* * * * *

At just a little after nine, Kevin and Bill climbed onto barstools and greeted Bruce, the bartender and bearer of a bowl of unshelled peanuts. "In another half hour or so, things should start picking up," Bruce stated. He looked at Bill. "Beer again for the two of you?"

Kevin added to the order, "And some information."

"I've talked to Steve," the bartender said, "and he's told me you're the man. I know of two more of the old crew who'll be here tonight, and they want to meet you too. Relax, drink some beer, and if you're hungry, remember that the tacos and dip are on the house."

"Beer and peanuts will do it, thanks," Kevin said and Bill agreed. Bud joined them at the bar and ordered a whisky sour.

Half an hour later, Bruce escorted two elderly men toward an office, and then motioned Kevin, Bud and Bill to come to the same door. Once the six men were inside, Bruce closed the door. "Customers can wait. We have some very old business to take care of."

Introductions were brief. Fred and Bob were introduced as old friends of both Stan and Steve, and the meeting was turned over to Kevin, who announced, "Twenty-five years ago, Stanley was knocked unconscious, repeatedly stabbed and left to die. A dedicated Bedford detective named Mike grew determined to solve the case, but the investigation, only a month and a half old, was stopped in its tracks by the anti-gay Bedford Chief of Police. Records were misfiled, and the case was pretty much forgotten, except by his family and the friends he had made here at the bar."

"We knew about that bigoted police chief," the man named Fred stated. "A lot of the fellows from Bedford were afraid of him and felt they needed to hide their orientation in that town."

"And that need to hide might be a part of this puzzle. Bill and I, Mike the retired detective and Nick the new police chief."

"And Kevin's dear wife Cathy," Bill quickly added

".We've formed a team, along with Bud, an openly gay cop, to find the killer and bring him to justice." Kevin waited to see if there would be a reaction to his being outed as a heterosexual and to the fact that he was married, but there was none. "We have very good information – based to a large extent on what we learned from Steve – that Stan had hooked up with a very possessive and controlling individual, who went into a jealous rage. He probably killed Stan and threatened the life of Steve."

"And that's what scared him off," Bud added. "Steve no longer felt safe here."

"We want to learn as much as we can about that man: the one Stan was seeing. We don't even know his name or where he is, so we're asking for your help."

"All I know is his first name," Bob said. "He shows up here once a year for our memorial gathering, but he doesn't socialize. Once the minute of silence is over and the sign comes back on, he's gone." There is no doubt in my mine, I'm sure he'll return this year as well."

"What's his first name," Bill asked.

"Jeff."

The J, Kevin said to himself.

"I know he's a tailor," the Fred shared, "and I think he still does alterations at the men's clothing store in Bedford."

Scissors, needle and iron, Kevin silently checked off his mental list. He added out loud, "My wife has also learned that he probably went to work at the men's store after closing his tailor shop."

"I'll never forget the night," Bruce stated, "when this guy had too much to drink and blabbered on about how his entire family had disowned him. I don't know if that was because he was crazy or because he was gay."

The conversation turned to Steve's life in Florida. Bill thanked everyone, Kevin promised to keep everyone posted, and Bruce again offered free tacos and dip before excusing himself to check on customers. Bill and Kevin finished their beers and waved goodbye to Bruce, Fred, Bob and the two coffee shop cooks, Ted and Larry, who had come into the bar after the private meeting began. Bud stayed on to socialize.

It had been a productive night, given the new information provided by Stan's friends. Having acquired a first name, Kevin had also confirmed that the man named Jeff was a tailor. He also knew where he was currently employed. He would share this information with the rest of the team in the morning.

Cathy was sleeping when Kevin got home, but she woke when he crawled into bed.

"I've been thinking about you. I'm glad you're home." "Bill outed me tonight. I told them I have a wife. Now they probably think I'm bi."

"Shhhh. The alarm's on, the coffee pot's set, and right now all I want is to snuggle and go back to sleep."

"We'll talk in the morning."

Chapter Fourteen

Over breakfast, Kevin excitedly filled Cathy in on all he had learned at the bar.

"So, it seems that we were in the right ball park with our interpretation of the scissors and stuff," Cathy said.

"And with the initial J."

Laying down her fork, Cathy looked at Kevin's unshaven face and asked, "Does this all mean that Margaret really did know the killer, and it's this tailor named Jeff?"

"Right now it looks that way, but nothing seems to be clear-cut, so I'm not holding my breath. We'll see with this morning brings."

* * * * *

By eight o'clock the team had gathered. Bill was introduced to Bud, Mike and Chief Harris. Everyone met Cathy. The six team members sat at a round table and everyone waited for Kevin to start. He filled them in on what he and Bill had learned at the bar. Then the Chief took over.

"Two officers in plainclothes will pick this Jeff guy up at the men's clothing store when it opens at nine. He'll be told it's about some old parking tickets that might or might not be his. At about the same time, I will go personally with one uniformed officer, and we'll pick up Lester. I'll say it's about a disorderly conduct complaint that Kevin filed, and I expect Judith to raise hell. I've authorized Mike to question Jeff, and I'll be in another room questioning Lester. Kevin, you, Cathy and Bill can observe Jeff's questioning through a one-way mirror."

"Sounds great," Kevin commented.

The small radio the chief had clipped to a shirt epaulet crackled. "Strange sound," he remarked. Having pushed a button, he leaned toward it. "Chief Harris here." He released the button and heard only static. He tried again. "Harris here."

Again static was heard, but everyone in the room heard a woman's voice softly say one word: "Finally." She couldn't send an email, but she could use the police radio. They knew that today, Margaret would be in that observation room.

* * * * *

It was after eleven when an officer came and got Cathy, Kevin and Bill, who had been waiting in the station's small lounge. He led them to a door, practically pushed them into a dark room and quickly closed the door behind them. They were no sooner in when the florescent lights in the room on the other side of a one-way mirror flickered and went on. Bud, in uniform, walked to the table and placed a tape recorder in front of one of the wooden chairs.

The door behind them quickly opened and closed, and they turned to see Mike standing there. He spoke softly. "An officer will bring Jeff in and read him his rights. I think he already knows this is not about traffic tickets. After the officer leaves, I'll wait a few minutes to let him stew a bit. Then I'll go in and tell him why he's here. We'll go from there."

He did not wait for any of the three to respond. "I want to tell you this, so you'll not be surprised. Jeff's fifty-five years old. Get this: his last name is Bailey. I asked him if he was related to Lester Bailey and he flatly denied even knowing the former chief. There are a number of unrelated Bailey families in Bedford and scattered around the county, so this could be sheer coincidence."

Just then Bud came into the lighted room, followed by a heavy man with salt and pepper hair, followed by a second officer. The suspect glanced around nervously, focusing on the mirror. "Am I being watched?" His question was audible over the speaker in the observation room. Looking up, he apparently saw the microphone hanging from the ceiling.

"Have a seat here at the table," Mr. Bailey." It was the chair facing the mirror. The recorder was placed on the table in front of Jeff, who squirmed nervously. "All or portions of this interview could be observed, but you will be recorded at all times." The officer turned on the recorder.

"What's this all about?" Jeff asked, his voice wavering. His anxiety became evident as he looked around the room that was bare of everything but the table, two chairs and the microphone hanging from the ceiling.

"The detective will explain all of that to you," Bud stated, "but I want to first ask you if you are aware that you are being recorded?"

"Yes," was Jeff's only response.

"Then I want to read you your rights." At that point the officer slipped a card out of his shirt pocket and read Jeff, verbatim, his Miranda Rights. When he finished, he asked, "Do you understand?"

"Yes."

"Do you want to call an attorney?"

"Not until I find out what the hell's going on. Am I under arrest?"

"Detective Miller will arrive in just a minute or two, and he'll explain everything to you." At that point the officers left. Jeff sat wringing his hands and staring at the mirror.

Mike picked up a phone in the observation room and pushed a button. "Someone distract the man in room C. He's focused on the mirror, and I need to slip out of here without him seeing the hallway light when I open the door."

Within a minute an officer walked into the room with a glass of water in his hand. When Jeff looked at him, Mike opened the door just wide enough to slide out. "I brought you some water," the officer announced, and left.

A minute later, Mike walked into the room. Without a word, he sat down in the chair opposite Jeff and broke the silence with a question. "What is your full name?"

"Jeffrey Allen Bailey."

"And where do you live, Mr. Bailey?"

"Here in Bedford in the Sycamore Street Apartments, Building X, Apartment Seven."

"The maple syrup X," Cathy whispered. Bill looked bewildered, but Kevin nodded.

"Do you live alone, Mr. Bailey?"

"Yes."

"Do you have family here in Bedford?"

"No family anywhere."

Just then the door to the observation room flew open, and Lester Bailey charged in, followed by Chief Harris, who was grabbing for him, and Judith, who was yelling almost as loudly as her father.

"Make her stop! Make her stop screaming! Make her stop, Jeff!"

"Shut up, Father," Judith yelled.

From the interrogation room, Jeff saw light on the other side of the mirror, heard all the commotion and spotted everyone in the observation room. "Get out of here," he yelled. "You don't belong here. I don't know any of you."

The whole time Jeff was yelling on one side of the mirror, Lester yelled on the other.

"Make her stop, Jeff. It's your evil. It's your fault!"

Added to this verbal barrage were Judith's pleas to her father to stop and to the others to not listen to him.

Then adding further to the ruckus, three uniformed officers crowded into the observation room, at which point Chief Harris ordered Lester and Judith to follow the officers to the interrogation room or be dragged there. They followed, but not quietly.

Cathy, Kevin and Bill watched intently as Lester and his daughter were literally pushed into the lighted room where Jeff was now on his feet. Chief Harris followed, and the three officers backed out. Miranda Rights were quickly read, the tape recorder was pointed out, and Jeff was ordered to sit back down, for he was heading for the man he now called "Father."

Out of the blue, Mike asked Jeff, "Did you murder Stanley Morgan?"

Jeff began to sob. "I loved the man."

"Evil!" yelled Lester.

"Shut up," yelled Judith at her father, and the tape recorder kept on recording.

"Did you kill him?" Chief Harris asked Jeff, repeating Mike's question.

"I could not kill him. I loved him, and I still love him."

"You've evil. You can stop the evil. You can make her stop screaming!"

"Who's screaming?" Chief Harris asked.

"She's screaming. She's evil. They're all evil." His arms flailed wildly.

Kevin had to get there. He had to be in the thick of it as things unraveled. He rushed from the observation room into the interrogation room. He knew it was Margaret's spirit screaming, but he suddenly wondered if Lester really knew that. "Who is the evil she? Who is screaming?" he asked.

Lester pointed directly at his daughter. His whole body shook. "She's the evil one. Make her stop screaming. She won't stop!"

Judith ducked her head and covered her face with her hands, as though she would be able physically to fend off her father's fiery words.

"What did you do, Judy?" Jeff asked. He was within inches of her. "What did you do to my Stanley? You know how I loved him. What did you do?"

In a strong, defiant voice Judith declared, "Stanley was evil, and he was making you evil." She fell to her knees. "Forgive me, Jeff. It was for your own good." Despite her words there was no remorse in her voice.

"What did you do?" Jeff asked again.

"Your father and I had to keep you from the evil, but it was too late. That's why even after I eliminated Stanley, we cast you out of the family."

"You killed my Stanley?" Jeff knelt in front of his sister and she did not avoid his glare. "You, my own sister, you killed him! You killed him!"

"He was seeing another evil man, and I had to protect you from him." Her voice remained adamant. "But it was too late for me to save you from the evil. I came to your apartment, knowing he'd be there. He wouldn't leave when I told him to, and we argued. I hated his evil. I hit him with your iron and he fell to the floor. I grabbed a pair of scissors from your sewing table and I stabbed him. I stabbed him repeatedly." Her hand held imaginary scissors, and she made repeated stabbing motions. "I called Dad. He helped me get Stanley into the trunk of my car, and then we cleaned up the blood. We dumped him in an alley and let the evil flow out of him. We did it all for you, Jeff. We did it for you."

The maple syrup scissors took on new meaning and the coroner's description of wounds from a thick blade now made sense. An iron would leave an impression resembling a garden spade. Kevin, the man, had to be there as the final puzzle pieces fell into place. "Oh, my God, I have cried for twenty-five years, thinking that some hate-filled stranger attacked Stanley in an alley." The anguish in Jeff's voice was palpable."

"And *you* wrote the notes to Steven?" Kevin asked Judith, who looked defiantly pompous.

"Yes, I did. That man was part of the evil. He was part of the reason I had to kill Stanley."

Lester stood quietly, listening to his daughter confess and implicate him as an accessory after the fact. For the first time in almost a quarter of a century he was calm. "It's over," he sighed. "She's finally stopped screaming."

Mike, Kevin and Jeff all sobbed. On the other side of the mirror, Bill and Cathy held each other and cried.

Having called in uniformed officers, Chief Harris instructed them to lock up Judith and her father in separate cells. He then cautioned Jeff not to leave town.

Wiping tears from his eyes, Mike mumbled, "Those two are crazy."

The room grew quiet, and Kevin gained some composure. "Speaking of crazy, don't ask me how I know, because I can't explain this. The image of peanut shells scattered around on the floor flashed through my mind. I have this strong feeling that we all need to be at the bar in Findley tonight. This is somehow important. It's as if we've all been living a novel, and there's just one more chapter."

"What time?" Mike asked. "I'll be there."

"Me too," Chief Harris said. "We have to finish this."

"I need to be there too," Jeff stated. He looked around as though fearful that he would be excluded.

"Of course you need to be there," Kevin said.

Bill and Cathy entered the room, each committing to the meeting.

"What time?" Mike asked again. He directed his question to Kevin.

Cathy went to her husband's side and waited for his response. He hesitated. His eyes focused on space, as though he were studying an image. "There are seven colors in the rainbow at the Rainbow Coffee Shop and seven colors in the Gay Pride flag hanging over the bar . . . "

"And I live in Apartment Number Seven," Jeff contributed.

"And the name Stanley has seven letters," Cathy added.

"We'll meet at seven," Kevin declared, to no one's surprise. "Bruce should be there, but he might be the only one. We'll meet at seven for the final chapter.

Final Chapter

With perfect timing, the six team members, Kevin, Cathy, Bill, Bud, Mike and Chief Harris, drove into the parking lot of the gay bar in Findley. Jeff pulled in as they were collecting at the bar's door. Kevin did not know what to expect, but he felt right with regard to being here. It was right that Bruce, the bartender, be a part of whatever was going to happen. Kevin was thrilled when they walked in and found that the two coffee shop cooks, Ted and Larry, had preceded them by only five minutes. There were greetings and hugs all around, with even Nick, the Chief of Police, getting into the act.

The outside door opened, and a balding, bespectacled man walked in and looked around. Ted spotted him first. "My God, it's Steve." He, Larry and Bruce ran to the man, who became the center of a group hug. They then brought him to meet the team, introducing Kevin as "The Man."

Steve went to where Jeff had remained seated. "I know how you loved Stan, and I loved him too. But my love had turned to loving him as my oldest and dearest friend. I would not for the life of me have come between you two."

"I was jealous, but I didn't kill our Stan, and I wasn't the one who wrote the threatening notes. My crazy sister did all that – she and my damned father, who had rejected me and covered up for her."

"Jeff, I heard some of that on the news, as I was coming in from the airport. I could fill in the rest of the story. I know you didn't hurt him."

"But after all these years, how is it that you picked tonight to come back, and to come to the bar just as we were meeting?" Kevin decided that this had to be more than coincidence.

"I looked through a scrapbook this morning, and came across a brochure Stan and I had printed up to celebrate the opening of our coffee shop. I must have looked at it a hundred times over the past twenty some years. Now this will sound crazy, but this morning I noticed a note in Stan's handwriting. It said, Meet me and our friends at the bar tonight, promptly at seven o'clock, and it was signed *One of the two Ss.* But I smudged the ink, which was fresh. So I knew immediately that I had to be here, even if I was five minutes late."

"You were always the late one," Larry teased.

"And we didn't want to sound crazy," Ted said, "so we didn't say anything. But mixed in with the customer orders for breakfast this morning, there was a note with the same message telling of a meeting at the bar at seven. It was clear to us that the story was ending, but not our endless love. On our way over here, we too heard the news about the former chief's daughter killing Stan, and how the chief covered her tracks."

"Guys," Cathy said quietly, "look over there." Everyone turned in the direction of a dim corner and became speechless. There stood a young woman and a young man, and between them stood a boy with curly blonde hair, who wore corduroy knickers. Everyone knew that it was Margaret and John, and between them was standing the only child they could ever have.

"Unbelievable," was wide-eyed Bud's only comment.

As they watched in amazement, the three visibly aged, the boy stopping the process when he seemed in his forties, but his parents continuing until obviously reaching their nineties. Each then raised a hand and waved goodbye, and Margaret blew a kiss that all in the room felt on their cheek. Then father and mother each took one of their son's hands, and the images faded into nothingness.

"After a quarter of a century, they're finally all together," Kevin said, tears streaming down his face.

"And Margaret is finally free to go with them," Cathy added between sobs.

"I thought I'd be happy finally to get closure," Jeff said, "but I'm hurting so much right now."

Bill put his arms around Jeff. "You have friends here at the bar. Don't stay away."

The neon beer sign flickered. Bruce spoke softly. "Let's have a minute of silence, so we can remember Stanley Morgan, each in his own way."

The neon sign went dark. A minute later it flickered, came on briefly, and then sparked. A puff of smoke rose from the connection of the electrical cord and neon tubing, and after one final flash of light, the sign went dark. "It's done," Bruce said. "It's finished. I think we have been told that it's now time to let go. It's time to move on. We'll not do the memorials here anymore."

"But we'll each remember something about this man and his very special family," Kevin said.

"And we'll each remember something about you," Mike said, placing his hand on Kevin's shoulder. "The man."

Hugs were exchanged, with the gay and straight men holding each other. Cathy kissed each on the cheek, and Mike was able to sneak one on her lips.

It was a good ending. The killer and accomplice would be brought to justice and Margaret was finally free, and finally the family was together.

* * * * *

"But what of the novel you want to write?" Cathy asked as they drove home. "Surely there's something in all of this that gives you a place to start or a character to develop."

He reached over and placed his hand on his wife's leg. "I have decided not to write fiction. My book will be on traveling through life accepting all of our neighbors, regardless of the color of their skin, their religious beliefs or their sexual orientation."

"I'm sure Margaret Ann would approve," Cathy replied.

Just then an approaching truck flashed its headlights as it drove on by and out of sight.

"She does," Kevin stated. "She certainly does."

ABOUT THE AUTHOR

Robert W. Birch is a retired psychologist. After his retirement he became a prolific author and poet. Bob has 34 published books, including adult self-help manuals, naughty and nice novels and short stories, and collections of poetry.

Bob's works can be found by visiting his Author's page on Amazon.com (search Robert W. Birch). Many of his books can be found also at www.erotic-romance-novels.com.